AFTER THE FLOOD

First Published in Great Britain 2017 by Mirador Publishing

First edition: 2017

A copy of this work is available through the British Library.

ISBN: 978-1-912192-40-3

Mirador Publishing
10 Greenbrook Terrace
Taunton
Somerset
TA1 1UT

After The Flood

Janet Killeen

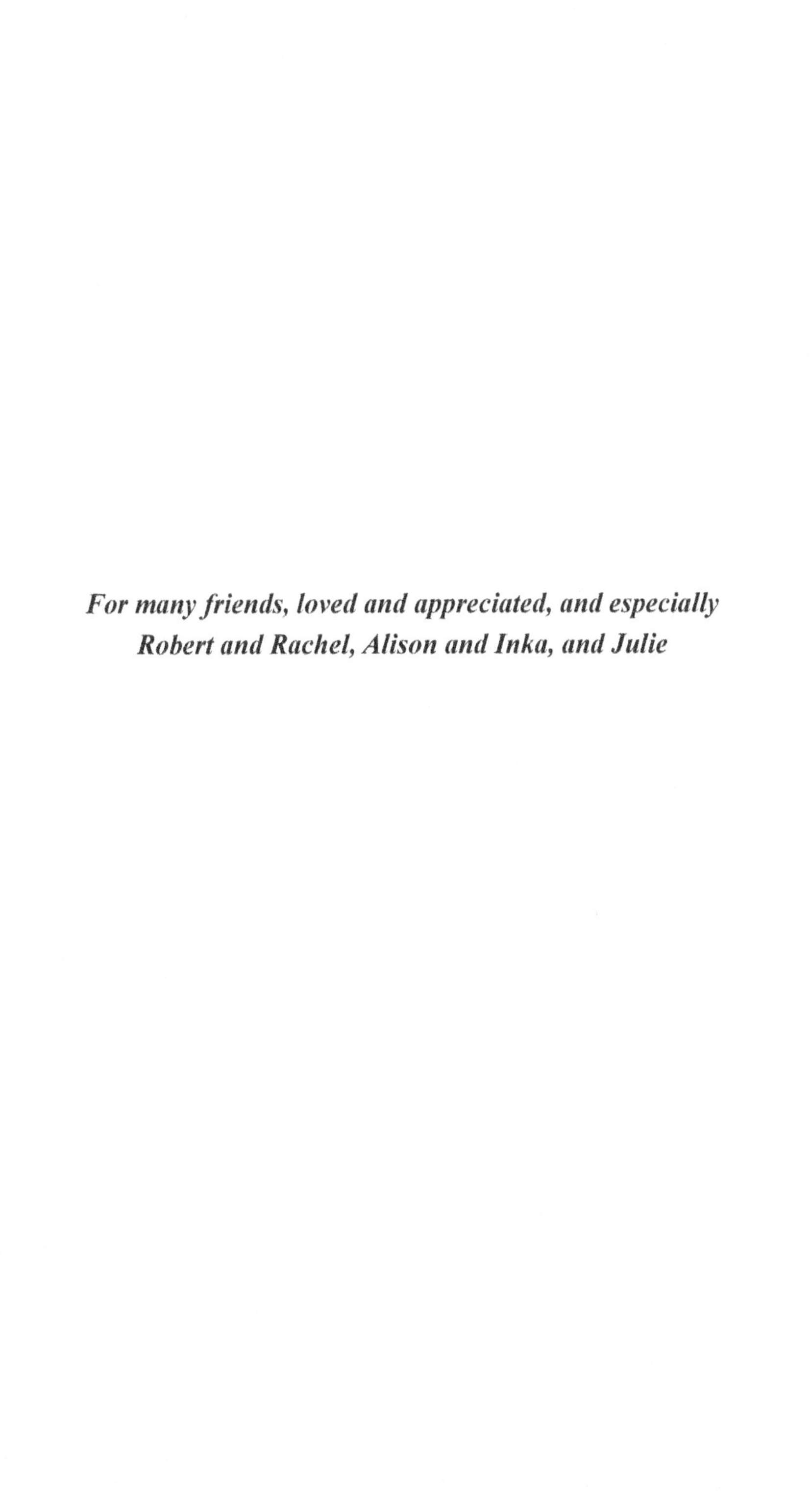

For many friends, loved and appreciated, and especially
Robert and Rachel, Alison and Inka, and Julie

Chapters

Chapter One	**Theresa**	**9**
Chapter Two	**Theresa**	**19**
Chapter Three	**Theresa, Adam**	**27**
Chapter Four	**Francis**	**43**
Chapter Five	**Francis**	**63**
Chapter Six	**Francis, Julia**	**81**
Chapter Seven	**Julia**	**94**
Chapter Eight	**Francis, Sidney**	**104**
Chapter Nine	**Amos, Thomas, Will**	**131**
Chapter Ten	**Will**	**143**
Chapter Eleven	**Amos, Thomas**	**149**
Chapter Twelve	**Theresa, Tony, Adam**	**158**
Acknowledgements		**187**

Chapter One

Theresa

Theresa smiled at him and he hated her. Hated what he sensed she instinctively knew. What he had resisted with the very essence of his being: the enduring absurdity of love.

Without speaking, he turned to climb the steps to leave. She lingered for a little. Something had changed. Some sense of raw and despoiling violence had violated this quiet space. Something even more damaging than the incursion of flood water all those months before his visit.

***

For countless weary days, unrelenting rain had drenched the land. The river levels had risen stealthily, until they bulged and spilled over their banks to run unchecked into waterways that in their turn, brimmed and broke free from their margins, engulfing all in one blank plain of water. A drowned wilderness: a waste of water, grey, unless the reluctant sunlight caught it. It lay deceptively calm, featureless, except for stark trees and besieged houses.

Theresa had watched the news footage, dramatic at first,

then, as it became an afterthought which trailed the main news as other crises occurred, until it was forgotten and the land and its people were left to draw on their own powers of restoration. Though she was separated from the sodden land and its stench of rot by the taut control of the television screen, the dread of its devastation filled her, and sometimes seemed to saturate her thinking with wordless fears. It became for her a sign of the imminence of loss, of some shapeless dread that she could not fully name. Yet she could identify some of what she feared: the house, that had become for her a place of hope, of connection, that house now might be ruined. When she closed her eyes she sometimes saw it swamped and drowned beneath the waters. And that other fear, which she had lived with for so long now that it had almost become as familiar as breath: the fear that, like the invasion of the land by these waters, so change would sweep away the ground of her past and all that she believed was her security.

Her husband, always pragmatic and considering only the financial investment, had rung the estate agent from London in February and requested that they commission a surveyor to make a preliminary, if necessarily superficial, assessment of the house. The report had been reassuring. Limited damage, mostly confined to the drive and gardens with a possible incursion of water to the cellar. Reassuring enough for Tom to delay their visit to the Southwest until the weather had significantly turned and they could take what action might be needed to restore any damage and air and clean the place. He was busy, preoccupied with the early spring rise in sales, and she hid from him the anxieties about the house that she knew he would readily dismiss. That other fear, that knowledge of what would come, must come, she did not speak of.

So, after the floods receded, long after the first signs of

spring, she and her husband and son returned together, to make the house habitable again. Perhaps: she did not dare give voice to her uncertainty. The house stood on a little rise, a brow, above the surrounding Levels and as they arrived in the early afternoon of an April day, the saturated land and channels caught the sheen of a cold sun, silver grey among clouds. Lank fingers of neglected willow trailed dripping beside the water.

The building stood, a mixture of honey-gold stone and red brick, with several brick chimneys and a cluster of small windows, much as it had done for centuries, though its stable, cowshed and barn had long since fallen into ruin and only traces remained. It had stood, she sometimes liked to imagine, waiting for them. That was how it had seemed to her when they had first seen it, two years before, and when it had caught at her heart. Yet she had visited countless houses in her working life. Visits with clients to whom she had shown properties, seeking to charm them as prospective buyers with her account of their distinctive features, whilst knowing intimately that they were but brick, stone, cement, foundations, and plumbing. Only this one place had ever held her, its uniqueness making her vulnerable. It appeared unchanged, even now, as they drove up and parked, though they saw that the water had brought a curdled tidemark of mud and debris up through the garden as far as the stone steps. The waters had not reached so far that they had penetrated the front door at their head: the green-black stain had lapped only the first step. But below the visible line of the building, they had been warned that the floods might easily have found an entrance to the cellar and sapped and damaged the foundations.

As she lay awake, much later that night, she remembered how long it had seemed that she had waited, her hand resting on the opened car door, looking at the house, hoping, yearning – she could not find the word for her feelings – that they would find all well when they entered. And the unspoken dread that it might be otherwise. Then Tom impatiently got out of the driver's seat, and Adam more cautiously from the back, and they had walked up the drive together. As always, she had dressed with care. The clothes were selected for a rural lifestyle: the pastel blue Wellington boots with their casual design of spots, the waterproof jacket with deep pockets. Tom, too, was bluff and confident in his wax jacket, cords and boots. Only Adam seemed to have no sense of a part that must be played. His hands were jabbed tightly into the pockets of his faded jeans; his grey-blue T-shirt and hooded sweatshirt so lacked colour that they seemed to merge into the washed blue of the sky, the dull sheen of the water. Together, they climbed the flight of steps, unlocked and opened the door and halted as, for a moment, a gust of stale, damp, unused air seemed to push them back, like a hand raised against them.

Theresa had prepared a thermos and food so that they might to pretend to picnic should there be no electricity, but they found, as they entered, a surprising normality. The plugs in the kitchen worked and she planned then to make hot drinks and later, offer something to eat, so that they could sit together around the kitchen table after their long drive and assess what was needed. She had brought simple necessities and bottled water, in case the water was undrinkable from the taps, but it ran clear and she began to fill the kettle. Looking around, she realised that her husband had already gone upstairs, checking the lighting and water, and opening windows to the chill brightness of the day. Adam lingered with her for a little while, and then, humming gently, wandered away to seek his room and his familiar and ordered possessions. She understood how much he too must have struggled to contain his fear; the fear that he would find disorder in this place, which of all the places he had ever known, had become his sanctuary.

Calling to them both a little later, she brought them back to the kitchen, to hot soup and rolls and fruit, and they discussed what they had found. The house itself, cold and damp though it was, seemed to have escaped structural damage, though this must be checked and confirmed. The wisdom of its builders, centuries ago, had raised it above the plain on a natural crest and set it up on a course of stone and brick foundations that lifted the floors and stairway higher than the level of the ground.

That afternoon was spent airing and warming the place. They lit fires with damply reluctant wood and coal in dusty hearths, and opened windows to freshen the sour air. Curtains were shaken out and clothes and linen collected and packed to be taken away to be laundered and dried. They did not linger beyond the early evening. As the pallid sun slipped indistinguishably into cloud and the twilight gathered around them they packed the car, closed up the house and left. Urgency, even a strange panic, gripped them and they found themselves glad to leave, thankful for the anticipation of the light and warmth of the hotel they had booked some miles away in Sherborne.

They talked a little in the car, mostly of their plans for tomorrow, expressing their relief that all was well. But later, when they had changed and come down to the bar and then been taken to their table for dinner, she sensed, as she picked her way with a diminishing appetite through the meal, that Tom had already turned away from their concerns here and would, within a day or two at the most, be gone. As she said that within her mind, the words ran on: *Be gone from me. From us*. And what she had known for many months, perhaps much longer, was at last admitted and given the validity, and yes, the relief, of words.

The evening faltered. A bottle of wine shared. Courses were served from a menu studied with something like desperation. 'Enjoy,' said the waiter, meaninglessly, as he moved away from their table. Then, they attempted some explanation for Adam of what the days ahead might hold as they came towards the end of the meal. They returned to the bar afterwards to engage in some casual conversation with local people who told a little of the events of the past months, shrugging away their stories of survival, much as their forefathers had done through centuries of flood and storm. Before long, Theresa and Tom walked with Adam to his room, and then at last to their own.

'I must get back, Theresa. You know that, don't you?' He smiled, speaking to her as he came from the shower room, still to her unique vision, dearly, even vulnerably familiar in pyjamas, rubbing his hair with a towel. Strange how the mind and heart would suddenly clench with feeling, with memory, despite all the years of growing separation. 'I've got contracts on hold because of this. They won't wait beyond Thursday night. Whatever you need, whatever expense, don't hesitate. This was your dream, and Adam is happy here. I want you to be happy.'

The rehearsed but not insincere phrases of departure were spoken. Conclusively. She recognised afresh the tersely punctuated words, a pattern of speech that had never left him. A pattern that had captured her, as a young woman, with its staccato promise of action, its eagerness and energy. There was still that edge of snipped vowels, sharp with city streets, concrete angles and corners. As she listened, she knew, she had known for years, though denying it to herself, that his business life and all that accompanied it had overtaken everything else. Probably there had been affairs, certainly there was a pace of living, a materialism, a visible success that she could not, and now knew she would not, share. For years, while the girls were growing up, she had, chameleon-like, adjusted to every stage of the family's upward mobility. Clothes, manicure, accent, hair: she had imitated, learned, gained a kind of acceptance on the edge of the circle, parking the car with the other mothers and minders to collect her daughters from preparatory school and taking them on to activities. They, unlike her, had swiftly taken on the mores of their peers, with a casual sophistication that left her behind. At least, their assured entry into this circle of activities had left her heart behind: she had remained an outsider, a careful imitator. She wondered, and wondered often in the months that followed, when it was that the trajectories of their lives had first peeled away from one another.

She watched her husband prepare to climb into bed: the customary movements of a shared lifetime. He put his watch next to him on the bedside table and then remained sitting up to check his I Phone. 'I'll just go through the emails before I settle down. I won't disturb you.'

The warmth of him was beside her, yet untouchable, far away across the smooth stretch of sheets. She thought, *It will be his touch, the shape and feel of him, and the sound of his breathing that I will miss and remember*. The essence of him, the shared talking and laughter, the delight of those early days of encounter and marriage, those things had gone away years ago. She realised that she had grieved for them dully without ever naming her grief and there were no tears now. She would not cling to him or plead for a reconciliation, a second chance to make their marriage work. Nor would she blame or blight what they had once had with angry accusations and suspicions.

He was fair and generous, and now she fully understood why he had pursued this dream, this purchase of an Elizabethan farmhouse in Somerset that she had set her heart on. It had set him free, without guilt. And it set him free from Adam, this late-conceived son who had come to them bringing such complexity of need and behaviour. She turned away from him in the bed. She wondered at first whether he would make any fumbling, regretful gesture towards her but he switched off his light, shunted down, alongside but so far away, and his breathing quickly moved into the heaviness of slumber.

It was many hours before she slept.

The next day they returned, early, so that they could snatch all there was of daylight to check the house and garden and venture into the cellar to assess what more serious structural work might need to be done before the house was truly habitable again.

'I need to catch the train tonight: I can wait until nine o'clock, but I must get back. I'll leave you the car.' He did not add, "then we will meet and talk and settle this thing", but it hung between them and she saw Adam fling up his head with that instinctive knowledge that he had, that intuitive sense of the undercurrents of meaning. She hoped, as she sought to hold Adam's eyes with her own, that he knew also that she was to remain with him, and that this was his home, securely, permanently now, not just in the holidays or for brief weekends, but always.

When they first arrived that morning, they walked slowly round the outside of the house, seeing it now, no longer with that immediate and hopeful relief, but with a more realistic sense of the laborious demands of restoration. They saw how the flood had crawled up the ridge upon which it was built, tearing out the flower beds and leaving them gutted. Then, as it retreated, a blackened debris of plants and shrubs had been scattered on the lawn, and strewn across the paths. A dank stain on the stone and a darkly livid green scum delineated where the waters had stopped at the foot of their steps. Sobered and anxious they entered the house, and when they had set its windows open to the light and air, and lit fires again in the hearths, Tom and Theresa took torches and opened the cellar door, Adam restlessly following close behind them.

The waters had gnawed toothlessly at the foundations, mumbling at brick and stone, exposing the roots of the house. Their flux had swept through a forgotten, choked tunnel into the ancient brick-arched cellar, under what must have been the hall and living rooms of the dwelling. Pressing in, it had ground away at the tired mortar between the stone and bricks until at one end, between what could now be seen as supporting pillars, a dividing wall had partially collapsed. And now all that debris lay crumbled; saturated; ruined: and what lay behind was exposed, gaping like an opened mouth.

Beyond the rubble, a space of darkness, as thick and tangible as felt. Their torches probed it: blades of flickering light that met the blankness of a further wall and then dropped. Dropped to where an arc of tangled bones lay dry and yellowed on a stone ledge high above the water's traces.

Chapter Two

Theresa

For many moments they stood together motionless, the silent air made harsh with their breathing. Fear touched their necks with chill fingers, rose in minute prickles on the skin of their arms, and stampeded the thudding tempo of their hearts. Tom, moving first, reached out protectively to hold his wife and son and turn them from the grim evidence of death that lay rigid on a shelf of stone. Their torches wavered and shuddered and then refocused as they were compelled, each of them, to look again. This time, details seemed to leap out at them. The hinged gape of the yellow skull, eye sockets and jaw, and the small dome of another skull, nestled against the ribcage. The clutching, crooked hands of bone. The wisps of hair and clothing that even as they watched seemed to fall into dust. Theresa stirred, drew a deep breath. An immense and paralysing dread had fallen on them at first. The evidence of secrecy, of stark death, with its ominous suggestion of violence, murder, concealment, was there before them. But even as she forced herself to look, to focus on this cage of bones, she became convinced that this was not a recent burial. Her thoughts ran, suddenly fluent with instinct. Grim and harsh as it was, it was old, skeletal; history buried behind a wall and waiting for them, yet with no vengeful or resentful presence. She did not realise then, but the image of the entwined skeletons had interpreted itself to her subconscious mind as an icon, an emblem of protection and care. Once the initial terror, the fear of violent death and crime had gone, she would always remember and understand it in that way. As her initial horror diminished, she moved more freely and Tom with her.

'Come,' he said. 'Adam, Theresa, come with me.' And he brought them both out of the cellar and into the startling light of the late morning sun. Even as he brought them through the door into the kitchen, he was reaching for his phone.

***

The police came, urgent with blue lights and sirens, and then later the local press, who were eager for a feature that would differ from the sad daily repetitions of flood damage and reluctant insurers. Theresa and Tom told their story first to a serious young detective sergeant, describing to him the opening up of the house after months of disuse during the floods and then their discovery of the bones behind the ruin of the wall in the cellar.

Adam sat hunched in the corner of the kitchen, silent, his hands clenched so hard that his knuckles showed white against the denim blue of his jeans. Theresa moved to be beside him, to read, if she could, the tightly held turmoil of his thoughts and feelings.

Studying the family, both police and reporters would find little that they could highlight. A middle-aged, perhaps older couple, both of them stylish with a city smartness that was not belied by the expensive casual country clothes or the

Wellington boots in the porch. The woman, careful in her hair and make-up, her clothes coordinated, even elegant; the man, well-dressed, blunt in manner, confident, hasty. The son was younger than expected for such a couple: tall, slightly stooping, with brown hair that flopped over his face, and wide grey eyes that seemed startled, vulnerable, as though still shocked, as well they might be, by what they had seen in the cellar.

As Theresa responded to the questions, describing their discovery, she saw with great clarity, as she would always see, the little skull nestled within the curve of the ribs, the tender encircling of the adult skeleton around the bird-like frame of the child. The clothing that had covered them had been so fragile with the effects of the damp to rot and destroy, that at a breath, at the stirring of the air, it had collapsed into gossamer shreds and left them naked. Horror had at first imprinted their image on her mind. Later, she would find herself interpreting it, drawing around those stark bones some garments of kindness, a clothing of kinship.

Meanwhile, she sat with Tom and Adam, as far from the kitchen door as possible, glad of Tom's no-nonsense steadiness that demanded answers and helped her to stay calm for Adam's sake. Snaking cables led through the cellar door to where, below them, were the harsh lights of the investigative team and the robed pathologist tending to the remains. It was not long before there was news: a relief, yet a mystery beyond all their knowledge.

'The remains are those of a woman and child – hers I imagine – around two years old, a little boy. They are very old. They've been hidden for three hundred years at least behind that broken wall. You'd never have known if the floods had not come. There's no crime that we can investigate here.' The pathologist smiled with grim humour. 'More a case for the museum to take on: local historians might have some clues. There are some things I can tell you. The woman has some broken fingers. There was a blow to her head, and a stab wound to her chest. The child's head was crushed. The stab wound that killed her had first penetrated the child: the blade scraped his ribs as well as hers. From the position of her arms she was trying to shield him from whoever was attacking them. We also found a small leather bag of jewellery and a miniature painting – a young man. It might have been a locket. Looked like the remnants of the kind of clothes you'd see around the middle of the seventeenth century. Not my strong point, history, but a specialist will tell you. There's a crime here that's been unknown for centuries. But nothing that need concern us, or you, beyond a report to the Coroner when I've done a full examination and then we'll see who will want to trace the likely family and the story behind it. Probably, as I say, the local museum or English Heritage at Muchelney. After that, there'll be a process to get the bodies buried.' He was talkative, unlocked by compassion, and the young policeman was nodding, smiling now with relief that there was nothing that he needed to investigate further, nothing that lay beyond his confidence and expertise. The team was collecting its equipment and moving out of the house, and loading vehicles with cables and lights, boxes. Quietness began to gather itself around them.

'But a sad story,' said the pathologist, suddenly, looking up for a moment towards Theresa as he packed his bag. 'A pitiful thing to discover. So much love in those bodies somehow.' He moved deliberately towards the door. 'I must be on my way.'

The detective sergeant flipped his notebook closed and stood up, moving with them away from the cellar door in the kitchen and into the hall.

'Well, Mr and Mrs Henley,' he said, youthful yet grave in the formality of the official phrases. 'That all seems clear and there's no further cause for any concern or police investigation.' Then, unconsciously, he echoed the pathologist's mood. 'A sad business.' Then, more briskly, 'I'm sure the press would like to talk to you. We will move the bodies now. I expect you will want to get some building work done soon: we may just need a further day of access to take more photographs and pass on the information to the appropriate people. And they, of course, may want to come and see you to discuss any findings. Thank you.' He smiled and nodded to them as they waited at the door together. 'It must have been a severe shock to you. But nothing sinister, not in our time, anyway.'

They stood closely together at the door to watch him go and with him the two other police cars and the forensic team with their lights and cases of equipment. Then they moved aside for the men who were carrying with careful tenderness it seemed to her, those frail locked skeletons, lifting them up the cellar steps and out of the house to the waiting mortuary van. Tom remained still, his arm instinctively around Theresa, as hers was linked through Adam's. They remained in shock, silent, moved beyond words at those fragile remains and the raw elements of their story that had been disclosed. Only slowly, after the van and the police cars had driven away, and the noise of them was lost in the wide landscape, did they recover movement, gestured responses, an involuntary drawing together as they gathered to sit around the kitchen table. And then, eventually, words.

***

Some hours afterwards, when they had talked to the first eager reporter from the local paper and stood to watch him leave, they moved back to the kitchen and looked at one another across the table.

'I would understand if you didn't want to live here any longer,' Tom said, and looked questioningly at Theresa, concerned, aware of her and of their son; suddenly more aware of their needs and vulnerability than for many months, perhaps years.

'Oh, no. No,' Theresa answered him. 'Nothing that happened here can hurt us,' and she instinctively stood up and moved towards Adam to touch his shoulder. 'Whatever happened, it was long ago, and like the man said, full of love and pity. Those are the things that have lasted. Not the violence.' She got up to boil a kettle, needing to trigger the everyday rhythms that would carry them back to normality. Then she saw Adam and the tell-tale signs of hollowed darkness beneath his eyes, the swinging of his foot to and fro, to and fro, that presaged a relapse into panicked and chaotic behaviour.

'Come with me, Adam,' she said and drew him gently to the window where the light, once pewter in its dull shining was now turning to gold as the clouds gave way to a clear and azure evening sky. 'We're going to live here now,' she said, calming him. 'In future, this is our home, you and me, and we won't be going to live in London anymore. We'll get the repairs done in the house and you can start work on the garden to restore it.' She reminded him of the things he had grown to love in the two years that they had been staying here for holidays and weekends, the things that had stabilised his world and would now enable him to cope. She spoke steadily, rhythmically, reminding him of what they had learned together, of the coming of birds and the transformation of the seasons. 'Under the eaves, the swallows will soon come back to nest. And rooks in the trees over there. Within days there will be branches breaking into leaf. There is so much for us to do, you and me, to make this place good again, and make it home.' Under her hand the shivering tension ceased and he gradually smiled. She glanced quickly at Tom and was surprised, moved, shaken, to see his eyes full of tears. He turned away.

'We must get moving,' he said, abruptly. 'I've booked dinner at the hotel and then I have a train to catch.'

All through the meal they preserved the intimacy of strangers; courteous, considerate remarks about how long to stay, when to meet up in London and sort out what so ambiguously could be called "their affairs". There was no ill-will, just, she realised sadly, an enormous relief, on her side as well as his. He had struggled to maintain a marriage that meant little to him, especially now the daughters were grown up and independent. She had focused her care on Adam, and with new understanding recognised that his needs must have exasperated Tom so much that he had almost forgotten how to love the boy. She was glad that she had seen those moments of tenderness and regret before they had left the house.

She and Adam took him to the station, and then returned to the hotel. She had booked their rooms for several more days, planning to find some other, more relaxed accommodation until they could move back into the house. It would be some time before it would be aired and ready for them.

'Has Dad gone?' Adam asked suddenly. His face was turned to her, questioning but not afraid, she realised.

What could she say? Now eighteen, Adam was not a child, and she knew that the bleak monosyllables of the question held more than he was able to say at this moment. 'Yes,' she told him. 'We are staying in Somerset. Our home is here now, at the farmhouse. Dad will live in London, and although we'll meet up and see him sometimes, he won't come and live with us here.'

He nodded. 'I know,' he said, calmly. But what it was he knew, he did not say, but she guessed that his knowing encompassed all the difficult and distant years of their shared lives.

She found them bed and breakfast accommodation nearby in Langport, and over the next weeks they spent every hour of daylight at the house and watched the farmhouse come slowly back to its familiar self. The chilled and clammy air was driven out of opened windows and warmth restored so that it became comfortable and welcoming again. Furnishings and curtains were aired and, where necessary, replaced and the linen and clothes were returned to them, freshened. In the garden, Adam began to cleanse away the traces of the floods' destruction, digging out and painstakingly shaping and replanting flower beds, clearing the lawn and the paths. Sometimes he would come into the kitchen exhausted after hours of work, yet calmed and confident as though the stress that he had always carried was slowly falling away from him and leaving him weary but free. The local builders came to reset the steps and block up the source of the erosion of the wall in the cellar and put in place the necessary props to ensure that all was structurally sound. The de-humidifier hummed to itself for days and nights. Plaster was stripped from damp walls and replaced, and the walls were repainted downstairs, simply, with white. At the very end of April, Theresa and Adam were able to move back into their home.

Only the cellar remained closed, temporarily altered by a beam and Acrow props, so that the upper rooms could be declared safe despite whatever damage the flood water might have done to the foundations. In a few months, the insurer's surveyor would return to give his final verdict on possible structural weakness and they would know what, if any, further steps must be taken to restore the property. Now all was silent and dark beneath their feet, and had been rarely thought of in the busyness of repair and renovation of the house. But when the cellar's blank space was remembered, it was still freighted with the mystery of the entwined bones.

There was a mild flurry of interest about the discovery. The local press featured it, and tried to get a story from Theresa of an escape to the countryside and a cherished dream of a country cottage, but although they found her polite and pleasant there was little sensation for them to make a story about her life and choices. They also sought to magnify the horror of the discovery and again found that her compelling reaction now was pity, not shock or revulsion. So the story died: a frisson of a long-buried mystery, a vague human tale of a dream that had become – not a nightmare. Something else, Theresa realised. A story that was perhaps hers to discover, at least in part, but something so life-enhancing in its meaning and humanity that it would forever alter all her conscious thought.

A cluster of nameless bones, curved in an arc, the small rib cage collapsed within the casket of the greater, like a child in the womb again.

Chapter Three

Theresa, Adam

The weeks, then months, passed steadily. Theresa saw Tom several times to discuss their separation and a financial settlement. The legal details were still to be finalised. Each meeting was awkward, as though strangers were exhibiting to one another the intimacies of a lifetime, or intimates were separated by glass and could only mouth incomprehensible words to each other. But gradually a new avenue of openness grew between them, which discussion of the discovery in the cellar helped them to develop, and this rescued them from recrimination. As the legal process came to an end, there was no manoeuvring to gain advantage. She met with her daughters one day in London and felt again with sadness how distant they were, how sensible and unmoved about the pending divorce. 'We saw it coming,' they implied. She struggled to understand when and how her relationship with them had failed, and in what ways she had let them drift into independence. Why had she not tried to pursue them with concern, with interest? She had let them go, too enmeshed in her relationship with Adam to notice the ways in which they had taken their own paths and left her.

There was too, personal sadness as the reminder of Tom's departure came to her, sometimes extreme and piercing, as she remembered the early years of their lives together. Gradually, however, it came only at the end of the day when she was alone, and the acute pain of it was balanced against tentative delight in what she experienced as an awakening to life. She found herself so busy, so totally engaged, that she would end each day exhausted, but deeply satisfied, as each room was gradually redecorated. She saw, and sometimes believed she felt, the house revive under her fingers. Discoveries emerged, of panelling and plasterwork from other generations; blurred entwined initials and a date that had been carved under the lintel. The decorated, twisting Elizabethan chimneys were restored and the hearths opened so that fires could be lit to bring a gold and reddening dance back into the rooms. She felt a growing sense of a debt being repaid to the past, to its endurance and to its mystery.

In the garden, Adam worked carefully, meticulously, in the ways which gave him pleasure, creating patterns and order so that gradually all the traces of flood and ruin were removed. Day after day, he dug out the beds for replanting and cleared the paths. Then they ordered turf to replace the churned morass of what had once been a lawn. He hired a rotavator, and cleared the land to prepare for it. With an old heavy roller that he found in an outbuilding, he levelled the ground. Each day, she marvelled at the strength, the growth of confidence and energy that he found. This physical exhaustion was grateful to him, bringing him sleep and a deeper security than he had ever known. She found a book in the local library, and shared with him pictures and plans of Elizabethan knot gardens and herb gardens and saw his interest awaken as he planned to recreate their formal miniature labyrinths and then consider the rebuilding of the wall around what would become their kitchen garden.

She realised, watching him, how perilously close he could be to obsession and control: to the rigid strictures of his own ordained sect. But to grow plants, when nothing could be certain, where the pruning of twig and branch only brought forth more growth; where blossom would surprise each spring with exuberance and fancy, and fruit, of unpredictable size and colour and shape, was always susceptible to the waywardness of maggot and fly. These things would always prove the lavishness and unpredictability of life and might teach him gently that he could not control and order it, nor exterminate the enemies of growth. Later, as he gained confidence, she would discuss with him the possibility of apprenticeship with a landscape gardener, or at a plant nursery, but not yet. Formal education had so nearly wrecked him and she knew that even the practical, "hands-on" learning of an apprenticeship might be too soon.

But underneath everything, even as the cellar was being repaired and the traces of its damage gradually removed, she found herself remembering, wondering, trusting that there would be a time to discover, if it were possible, who the woman had been and when and why she had died. She asked the parish vicar to come and say a prayer where the woman and her child had lain for all those centuries of soft falling dust, not because there was any unquiet presence in the house, but because she sensed how abrupt, how severed from all piety and kindness, had been their deaths. And prayer, whatever it meant, she thought of as timeless, able to flow back and forth to the instant of their deaths and to the moment of their bodies' discovery. She did not know whether that wall had been built in shame and furtive concealment or in protection, to keep those cherished bodies safe from exposure and depredation. They lay together now in the churchyard, a small grave with a featureless stone inscribed that their identities were unknown and giving a possible date of death. She had been there, and Tom and Adam with her, and a few local people and representatives from the museum at Sherborne as the simple, ageless service commended them to the earth's kindness and the mercy of God. She imagined them now, mother and child, bound together in the folds of a simple shroud. It seemed to her that they were like a remembered statue of the Virgin, so worn and smoothed by time that the Infant was indistinguishable from the arms that held him. An iconic, simple shape, now clothed again. When the funeral had taken place, there was a recurrent flicker of brief interest in the local paper, and speculation about their names and the manner of their dying, but it soon fell away.

The season turned to early summer and warmth and sunlight brought an astonishing revival to a landscape that had been saturated, satiated with wetness. The meadows revived with golden, white and purple wildflowers, trees grew heavy with leaf, and the water lay tamed and sedate in the ditches that she learned to call "rhynes" and within the curving banks of the River Parrett.

From the local museum, she learned a little of the farmhouse and the bodies it had held. The skeletal remains dated back to the middle of the seventeenth century: probably the period of the Civil War. The miniature of the young man, his clothes and curled hair, and settings of the few jewels (held in a leather bag which had fallen to dust at a touch, however delicate) that had rested beneath her chin and the head of the child, all indicated a Royalist. And the young woman, Theresa was certain, was his wife, and the child so tenderly held was their son, who had been born, perhaps in the early 1640s. No trace of the husband's fate could be found, but the turmoil of the ensuing years of war could well have swept him up.

Perhaps, she thought, tentatively. *Perhaps if he had known of the fate of his wife and child, he would have been glad to have been lost in war's chaos and immediacy. To have no time to feel the unbearable weariness of sorrow when danger, life and death had to be confronted daily.*

She discovered a little of the early years of that war that had turned friend against friend, son against father. Until now, she had never thought of it, never realised that such a conflict had taken place, ripping a nation apart for a decade of war and grief. There was evidence to be found in damaged walls and the names of long-forgotten skirmishes and battles nearby. The towns of Sherborne and Yeovil had seen fighting, and Sherborne Castle had been besieged. Early in September 1642 the Parliamentary army had been forced to retire from Sherborne in disorder, and many deserted. Perhaps in that confusion the farm had been attacked and overrun, or the owner, already at war, had left his wife and child defenceless. What had happened to him, she wondered? There was no trace of him, save the serious yet appealing face of the man painted in miniature so long ago. Without that blurred record he might never have existed. And what of those who had come to attack the woman and her child? Had it been a lone killer, or a group? Did their actions haunt them, or was it seen simply as the spoils of war, the inevitable consequence when violence is let loose: the minor, insignificant, casual incidents of war? One of thousands that are remembered by no-one; that have no battlefield or campaign to commemorate them. It seemed to her a strange thing that battles and their buried dead should now lie forgotten, but a single woman and her child could speak so powerfully of the cost of conflict: the nameless, casual deaths of the vulnerable in time of war. She would never know the truth of their lives: only live with an instinctive kinship that reached across the centuries to an unknown woman and her son, torn from life.

Theresa, with this fresh and painful engagement with a world beyond her own, wondered often how such terror could be endured. Yet she knew, even as she framed the question, that day by day it was being repeated endlessly by countless people in different places of conflict. Each day was bringing them the news of horror from the Middle East and the staged cruelties claimed as acts of devotion. Young men, young women, Adam's age, she realised, were drawn to it, to its stark ideologies, its unambiguous assumption of perfect righteousness. She could see that obsession, that a detachment from empathy, could draw Adam into such simplified beliefs were it not that she tried ceaselessly to keep open the communication between them through the things that he loved. At the back of her mind these thoughts, this sense of moving between strands of time that ran in parallel, stayed with her as she followed what few lines of research were open to her.

The farm had once been a small manor house, most likely belonging to a younger son of the local Phelips family, loyal to King Charles in a conflict which had left ruin and poverty behind it in much of the West Country. There was little trace of it recorded after that period. The outbuildings had fallen into decay; the land abandoned or sold off in lots: no heir, no claimant. Later it was bought or taken and turned again into a small farm, and the Elizabethan house reshaped a little into more classical lines for the new eighteenth century and inhabited, though not with any clear line of descent, until it had come onto the market three years ago, and she had seen it.

She had seen it on a transparent day, the air cool, still, holding its breath. They had driven down from London with the object of house hunting.

'Our country retreat,' they had said, mocking the words' pretension, in the days when there were still jokes between them. She had hardly dared to dream of it: knowing that it was her heart's desire, knowing that in some mysterious way it could be a home for this beloved son of hers who could find no way to settle or heal in London. They planned to stay in Shepton Mallet, to explore the area further west, but they had found this: a chimneyed house of golden stone and red brick on the crown of a small rise. Meadows, knee high with greenness and the sparkle of wildflowers. Birds, as yet unknown, calling and circling above the meadows. The lane ran beside a channel of still water, and crossed it on a narrow stone bridge as they turned up the rough driveway. A tilted sign on the tree at the gate. "For Sale".

Tom's immediate willingness to press ahead with an offer had surprised her at the time. They had returned to the estate agent, whose office lay beyond Yeovil in Sherborne, and talked together, all the old eager language that reminded her of the excitement of their shared business in the late seventies and eighties. He, energetic, out in all weathers, negotiating, making connections, and she, the welcoming face in the office, working patiently to build client trust, to suit the property to the buyer, to keep the fragile links of selling and buying connected. She remembered how much they'd shared of the planning and risks, and then, of course, Sophie, the first of their girls came and then the second, Emma, and she had withdrawn from the business to care for them. It had seemed to leap forward suddenly: a small local name becoming a chain, a brand, with customised cars and advertising on local radio. Then the new ventures into property: building, leasing, contracts. It had been – still was – a huge success. She had focused on the children, able to provide for them the kind of life and schooling that neither she nor Tom nor their parents could ever have dreamed of. Only after Adam was born when their eldest daughter, Sophie, was sixteen and her sister Emma three years younger, did the success seem tarnished by doubt and insecurity. Her husband was now so often away and the baby screamingly unsettled and no-one knowing why. The remembrance of those screams would still come to her sometimes when she stirred out of sleep, and she would momentarily re-live the long nights of wakefulness and the desperate desire to reach and comfort this flayed anguish, this desolation, that was her son.

The years since had been ones of imperceptible degrees of separation, not explicit, not expressed in any kind of words or acrimony, but Tom frequently came home late or went away on business trips and they had ceased to talk. They spoke, but never talked. The girls, Sophie and Emma, had done well, and she had shared with Tom all their achievements but so little of her struggles with Adam. What had happened to her, she wondered, as she looked back over the years? When had she begun to awaken out of the sleepwalking that had possessed her? And worse, had she lived always in a caul of complacency, absorbed and focused only on herself and her own? Now, was this just a dream home, like some television reality show of escape to the countryside? A desirable Tudor house, an acre of land.

She had left behind the routines of their London home, the predictable patterns established over the years. She had taken the girls to school each day, preparatory first, then private, and to the clubs and the music and dance lessons they had requested. She had been careful to conform to the new social expectations of their lives; the steady purchase of new houses in "better" areas, the attendance at concerts and Speech Days. Now, their daughters had grown and gone to university, the churning waters of their adolescence threaded without lasting mishap and they were well settled in the certitudes of their own lives - trainee solicitor, fashion buyer. Soon to be married, the younger. She and Tom would come together for that occasion and perhaps Emma would want her advice, her involvement in the arrangements. How different, she thought, from her own wedding so many years ago! A different era. She saw that there was an easy, undemanding relationship between her daughters and herself: but cool and even indifferent, she realised now with this new and disturbing questioning of everything in her life. They did not need her. Perhaps she had turned away from them too soon, too absorbed in the care of that troubled, late-born son to notice the moments when they might have forged a new bond as adult to adult. Moments that were gone now, she acknowledged, that had rushed away in the rivulets of their lives, heedless and busy. But now, suddenly, starkly, all was changed for her. When had she begun to awaken? Would she ever stumble over the threshold of life and death as that woman had, lying curved about her child, hidden and waiting in silent decay? Had she, that unknown mother, been jolted in that one instant into authenticity, into veracity? She recognised that this glimpse of another life, its stark devotion and simplicity, had changed all things for her. Terrors and misery, distanced by the regular calm detachment of television newsreaders, the edited glimpses of incomprehensible conflicts and languages, the impermanent headlines of newsprint, now rushed towards her, as inescapable and valid as these bones, that enduring, iconic embrace.

She had no lens to examine herself impartially now, only

seeing herself pitilessly, distorted, as in a convex mirror. She identified her total absorption in her family, her marriage and her son as exaggerated, defining blemishes: preoccupations which had separated her from all that might have drawn her into engagement with a wider kinship in the world. In the harshness of this self-examination, Theresa had no reassuring sense of how her life had long ago begun to move towards this enkindling moment. Yet it was so, and the whole course of her existence had led to this, although she could not recognise it.

Then one incident came back to her, like a simple torch to lead her out of a labyrinth of thought in which she might otherwise have lost herself in self-reproach.

It had been more than three years ago, and she had requested an interview with the headmaster at Adam's small, select, private school. His misdemeanours, the letter ponderously told her, were so serious that the school could no longer countenance them, and he was to be permanently excluded.

His ready handshake seemed sincere. He held it though, for a full heartbeat longer than was needed. She felt with unease the moisture of his palm, the flaccid pressure of his thumb. She withdrew her hand, focusing with care on the genial eyes, the tightening of the upper lip that brought his mouth into a smile and seeing the tiny bubbles of moisture that broke out on his temples. He sat. The desk lay wide between them. Photograph frames angled to show wife, child, child, dog. And another, a newer frame, the elder child graduating between proud parents. A stack of papers; a file to the right. Pens in a careful stand. A scoop of paper clips. Two telephones. He smiled again, the eyes shielded with heavy lids. The file moved under his hand to come directly between them.

'Adam,' he said, tapping it. 'You wished to see me.'

She felt the strength drain out of her. The tone disabled her. *Why, you fool, when you know how helpless you are. Why question my decision? You cannot win, you know.* Her childhood's half-forgotten denigration at school and loneliness at home, acquiesced. It was, of course, hopeless. How foolish of her. These people always knew best, always held sway. Her eyes dropped to her hands linked in her lap, but not before she caught for a second the glitter of mockery, the assumption of power in his eyes as he looked at her. Something deep within her cringed. Turned away from conflict. And turned again to look up and to speak.

'Yes, Adam. My son, Mr Griffiths. My son.' Her voice was riding on a column of air from her diaphragm, her mouth giving shape to her heart's expression.

'Yes?'

He remained calm, she saw that. Practised. Poised. His fingers touched the file delicately, fastidiously, as if its contents were unclean.

'Adam.' All her love in those syllables, all her struggle to provide for him and cope alone when she sensed that her husband was drifting away. She unfolded the letter. 'You say that this is the last of "many such misdemeanours" and there is no alternative but to expel him.' She paused. 'But there has been no previous warning given to me that he was in any danger of exclusion. No-one has told me of the things you speak of in this letter.'

'What you do not realise, Mrs Henley.' His mouth flexed around the words as he spoke: suave, measured, rehearsed phrases. He waited. Repeated. 'What you do not realise, is that a list of minor offences may suddenly be seen in a new light when such a serious act takes place. Your son broke all our rules, photographing a teacher on his phone in such a way that the photograph could have been used to humiliate her. You must agree that this goes far beyond what is acceptable or forgivable? I have a duty to protect.' He paused, sweeping his hands sideways as though to gather invisible persons into his care. 'I have a duty to protect my staff. I must make a clear example of this behaviour to our students.'

She saw him move backwards in his chair. His hands were recalled from their studied embrace of the vacant air and came together carefully to rest on the cover of the file, thumbs together, manicured fingers outspread. To crush what lay beneath, she realised: the interview was being brought to an end.

'No, Mr Griffiths, no!' she said, her voice harsh with an anger that was new to her, and her gasps of breath punctuated the words. 'No! He came to you with a clear assessment of his needs. He's received very little specialist support. This incident that you describe. A boy with a mobile phone. Other boys egging him on. The photo immediately deleted. A heartfelt apology. An act of immaturity by a boy who is unable to cope with the demands put upon him – the demands that he should achieve academically when he struggles to organise himself, to write coherently. Where is the understanding of his needs? What about your commitment to him?' She looked up, above his head, at the gilded badge on the wall, its spurious devices and motto, the book and test tube, the rainbow. 'And what about the values of your school, "Encouraging excellence for all"?'

The head teacher gazed at her, unmoved.

'I will take this to the governors. They need to see the disconnection between your careful marketing and your actual practice. How you treat a student who cannot reach your academic goals.' She mimicked his gesture of inclusive care.

'It's not the care of your staff or students that is your concern. It's the impact on the league tables, the percentage of top grades. The marketing.'

She realised even as she spoke that her words were like spray on rock. This man, his school and his governors were solid, rigid, against her. Nor could she imagine sending her son back into a system that would be inimical to him now. The hostility, veiled but obdurate, would crush him under their bland nods of acceptance even if she fought for his return. She waited, sensing the power of his seemingly mild, yet secure resistance and knowing it to be insuperable. She got up. He did not move.

'I will take my son elsewhere. Not because of your ruling, which is unjust and lacks all compassion, but because his needs are my priority and I will take him where they can be met.'

'That is as you decide, Mrs Henley. I think this interview is at an end.' He did not rise but remained behind the smooth polish of his desk. His hands shunted the file to one side even as she watched, even as she got up, and stood, her hand on the back of the chair. He left her to turn, walk across the carpet to the door, and fumble with its handle. Turning, opening, closing it behind her. Then she leaned for a moment against it to draw breath steadily, holding back the impulse to bend over, to gasp and cry.

And then she walked down the corridor, pushing through the doors, out, out into the car park and drove away. Only much later, safely at home, did she allow herself to react in tears with the mixture of rage and humiliation that she felt.

Theresa stirred. The inundation of memory had taken her by surprise, but she saw how critical, how transforming the experience had been. Her voice had risen out of her: decisive, certain. And from that time she had, almost without realising it, begun to make decisions. She had brought in tutors for Adam and worked with him herself, discovering how his restlessness, his fragile sense of safety and order, could be focused as he learned to do the things he loved, the things that brought him calm. She had talked with Tom about a house in the country, somewhere away from the stress of their London home. Daily, she saw her son made timid by the exuberance or potential aggression of crowds and the rush and heedlessness of traffic. Tom had agreed. A second home he considered to be a good investment. They could afford it. She realised now how it must have eased his path. There need be no confrontation, just a gradual separation until almost no words need be said, but she would be well provided for, and Adam. They had begun to search, taking time on Sundays to drive out into Surrey and then Sussex, then sometimes staying overnight as they began moving in widening circles towards the West Country. It was companionable, in a strange way, bringing back memories, old skills, shared knowledge.

She remembered vivid images from those searching journeys, instants of sight that seemed to have some power to lodge in the memory because they carried meaning. The lurching swivel of a troop of wind turbines, gathered on the flank of a hill. Their slow, unsynchronised rotation grinding the particles of the wind. A kestrel balanced on a plinth of air. She had felt, with a second's shiver, the unimaginable, scurrying terror of the vole beneath it. Then they moved through the ancient landscape of Dorset and between the hill forts which rose up, she thought, like the shoulders of lions. Ancient trackways were scooped into their flanks, trodden over the centuries by man and the beasts he herded, and the curves of rampart and ditch were softened by time and weathering, but not obliterated. Here, she had known with an instinctive certainty, here in the west they would find the home she sought. Where there could be connection with a deeper past, a wise endurance.

Then they had seen it: glimpsing the chimneys first, from a track branching off a winding lane as they followed the agent's direction, then the windows catching the light that gilded the mellow stone. She had known even before they got out of the car. At first they had only visited for weekends or short breaks in the summer months, Tom, eager to employ a firm for renovation and refurbishing to make all ready for them. The house was repaired and decorated, the grounds were to be landscaped and fenced and cleared of rubble from the abandoned farm buildings. A sound investment.

But then the floods had come, and a wall had collapsed between the past and the present, and the fragile beauty of those exposed bones was not a haunting, but a gift to her, and to her son.

***

On the Levels the pattern of life is ageless. The peril of flood in winter lasts until after the spring rains. The rain falls to soak the land and satiate the channels that had been cut long ago to carry the waters safely, and an accompanying swell of water in the river might overlap the fields, threatening to drown the good pasture. The willows, coppiced at the water's edge, stand stiff above the waterline. Water birds gabble and bob along the rhynes. Before the summer has ended, there had always been a need to clear the waterways of drifting debris and static weed so that they ran clear and could take away the bulging waters that might else engulf the land as autumn followed. Theresa had glimpsed the pattern, but until this crisis, had not seen its necessary rhythm, nor understood how closely her neighbours were attuned to the moods of the water. Attuned, as their ancestors had been, for even longer than the centuries that lay between her and the skeletal remains that the floods had revealed. Understanding now just a little of the pulse of the past, she thought of those who had lived here, in this house, those whose happiness had been so violated, suddenly and brutally, centuries ago. They would have walked the same lanes and beside these channelled waters, whose dormant currents ran imperceptibly beneath so still a surface. These timeless skies would have been wide and clear above them as they worked these fields and banks and walked together: yet their names and loves and hopes would always be unknown to her.

Chapter Four

Francis

Never to be known to her, despite all her research and enquiries. Names and lives as ephemeral as smoke, leaving only a stark anonymous calligraphy of bones that nonetheless wrote so clearly of timeless things: selfless courage, suffering, love.

***

Francis Phelips. Only son of the youngest son of a declining house.

Little left for me to inherit, he had thought wryly, as he took possession of the small manor and neglected farm that crested the Levels. *Yet enough.* Enough to bring home his new wife. Enough to pass on an inheritance, secure, to the sons they dreamed of, the daughters they would protect and endow. 'All my treasure will be here,' he had said aloud to her, as he lifted her over the threshold, shy and tender and excited both of them. He would always remember Nell, the maid, running forward and taking her cloak and her portmanteau as the coachman lifted down her small coffer, and John and Marjory bustling to prepare food and drink to welcome their new mistress. 'All my treasure will be here.'

A summer's evening. The light caught and lingered on the chain of the locket she had around her neck, her father's gift to them, a twin locket that unclasped to show them both, facing one another as it opened. Her father had brought a miniaturist painter from Salisbury to capture their likenesses and she wore it now. Stiff and a little formal, yet he had captured somehow something of the lilt and laughter of her mouth and eyes and the grave hopefulness of Francis' face. The sun was slipping towards the horizon, but its light flared crimson and gold along the waterways, and long traceries of shadows lay across the fields from the far trees. Such golden stillness, as though time had lost its way and would not call on them that evening, or perhaps for many days. Yet all their days were measured now, although they were unaware, by the trim footsteps of a man in the Palace of Whitehall, pacing out his destiny as he took the nation with him towards war.

Francis was the king's man, through long and unquestioned loyalties. So, despite all rumour of war and disturbance, that was settled for him. Ties of family fidelity; West Countryman; member of Exeter College. No other thought would ever come to him, despite the hard months of campaigning that would eventually lie in wait for him, despite his slow, despairing recognition of the desperate paradox of the savagery and gallantry of war. But that pending war was unimaginable to him now, in this moment of gladness. Just as it was unimaginable that King Charles, glimpsed briefly at court as a pale aloof face, floating disembodied above the dark crimson clothes and the finely worked lace collar, would let loose a war that would turn countrymen against one another, brothers and cousins, neighbours. Families and friendships, split as trees are rendered for firewood under the axe. Men who would strike at one another's bodies until the soil was reddened, the grass splattered, clotted and crushed beneath the dead. A small, elegant man, lonely under the burden of Divine Right that he carried, who seemed most at ease beside his wife and children: husband and father, not king at all. Sitting with them, as Francis had once seen him, watching the slow unfolding of the play, "The Winter's Tale".

But to Francis then, the affairs of the king and his increasingly defiant Parliament, a Parliament that had been dissolved for the past decade, were far remote. A distant shaking of the foundations that as yet barely trembled beneath his feet. He carried Julia to the window where they could look out over the land: to its lush pasture for hay and the calm, grazing cattle. It fell away before them to the lines of reed and willow that marked the rhynes that drained the Levels and held at bay the sweep of water that else might rise up in winter, or overflow from the River Parrett. Beyond the house, as he circled the room to gaze with her through each window, there were the beginnings of an orchard, planted with young, slender, stripling apple trees, with a south-facing wall for peach and apricot, and then an enclosed kitchen garden intersected with bricked paths. At the front of the house she could imagine a garden, small, but in imitation of their infinitely wealthier neighbours at Montacute House, a pattern of borders of pinks and carnations and roses trained over archways, and in the spring, perhaps there could be one day - who knows, she smiled to herself, knowing their cost - precious bulbs from Holland in ones and twos. She laughed inwardly with the unreal dream of it as she imagined that they might be garnered and planted to grow and multiply. And then, threading through the borders, love knots of low, box hedge. A lifetime's work, she knew, but already sensed in her hands the joy of it. And their children, living here, and their children's children. Shy but confident, she pressed her face against his cheek, shifting as he carried her to draw closer to him, clasping her arms more closely around his neck.

'I will never have wealth,' he whispered to her, whilst wondering silently, 'how can I ever give enough?'

'Love is enough,' she answered gently, wise beyond her years. She turned her face so that she might look at him and there were no words needed.

Later, and only for a brief, starkly contrasting moment, he remembered the stench of London in high summer. The gutters that congealed, stinking, along every street, the corners where men relieved themselves, the slap and belch of the Thames at low tide when the river ran brown and thick, with offal from the butcher's markets, with beast and human excrement and with rubbish of every kind, including the dead. Here, though, he could forget its foulness and its loneliness, and the prickling stink of it that had lingered uncleanly in the nostrils. In this quiet, he could forget the raucous, enraged voices, shouting and heckling around street preachers and the hatred that could name even the name of God with rage and tear one another with words. Here, in this place, there was air and light, and lightness of heart. He looked across the table at his wife as they ate together later, both pretending a hunger they did not feel to gratify their cook, Marjory, who had dressed their meal with such care. They were so grave and hesitant together, yet he felt as if bubbles of joy could burst from them if only they could escape from this formality. As the darkness gathered gently around them and the candles were lit, he took her in his arms again and carried her to their bedchamber.

Those early awakenings to contentment! He carried them

somewhere in his memory always, unviolated despite all that happened later. The sun would come slipping into their room as they woke to the warmth of shared breathing, to the laughter that followed passion, the tenderness that preceded it. In the minutes before they got up, her head lying against his shoulder, she loved to ask him about his past. She was piecing together the story that seemed to her to be miraculous, that he should remember her and choose to return to find her and settle here, so quietly, so far away from the life she imagined he might have had, a lawyer in London. And he would laugh at her and tease her a little, and each time begin:

'When as in silks my Julia goes,
Then, then, methinks, how sweetly flows
That liquefaction of her clothes.'

Sometimes the story would get no further and they would return happily to the secret wonder of intimacy, but sometimes he would tell her of his life, and slowly from those morning confidences, and more that she would draw from him as they walked together in the fields or beside the river, or over their supper in the evenings, she came to see how his days had made him who he was. Because she loved him and responded to him, as water is stirred by the slightest hint of breeze, she saw more in his face than he could tell, and understood him and how closely he had walked with loneliness.

***

His mother had died when he was five, in childbirth, and he remembered the stricken household, his father's grief and sullen despair, and still saw, or thought he did, the tiny body of the baby brought from the room, unwashed, bloodied and curiously inert, half wrapped in linen. And the doctor rushing up the stairs with mud-caked boots, and the maids crying. He recalled the parson coming, too late to bring comfort. All the time, he was in a watching corner fix-eyed with the dread of it, shivering in his nightshirt. Many days later, tearless with misery beside his rigid, angry father, he saw his mother buried in the churchyard nearby and hoped that her little daughter lay safely in her arms.

After that he grew up. He took his first Greek and Latin lessons with the parson, and then spent some years at the school in Sherborne. In the holidays, when he could be spared from haymaking or harvest, or from the care of the animals, he wandered the lanes and fields. Sometimes he met up with other boys from the family, cousins and half-cousins, but there were no brothers or sisters. Nor could there be, even though his remote, stern father married again, and his compliant wife Madeline struggled repeatedly to bring him children, weighed down with the weary gravity of pregnancy again and again. But no baby seemed to survive longer than a day or two in that bleak household.

Ten years or so after his mother's death, he went to Oxford. Like most West Country boys, he joined Exeter College, following in the footprints of relatives and neighbouring gentry. There, he found at first a world that overwhelmed him with its noise and boisterousness. Swaggering young men of sixteen and seventeen appeared to him to be gentlemen of sophistication and intellect and they seemed to argue, laugh, drink, wench and swear their days and nights away as though they cared nothing for the future. But he found ways of hiding from them, studying because there was nothing else that he knew how to do, and very gradually he discovered the outer circle of those who more seriously debated the religious and political issues of the day or talked about the poets and playwrights of the age. In those days of heady dissension, in 1627, as religion and politics dominated and divided the affairs of court, Parliament, cities and the two universities, there could be no escape from their imminence. Francis listened to men who argued fervently for their beliefs that the king had no right to extort taxes that were not agreed by Parliament; that he was not divinely appointed at all and was leading the country, together with his Papist wife, perilously close to Rome. In the marketplace preachers would risk the filthy pelting of a fickle multitude to denounce the Popish ways of the king and his court, and would declare that there was no need for man to have a priest to intercede for him with God. Francis wandered bewildered through streets that swarmed with students and past the enticements of girls, younger than him, who beckoned him to come to corners of whispered furtive pleasure that tugged at his groin. Sometimes the alleys thronged with the quarrels of young apprentices, cursing and envying the students who outdid them by their dash and swagger and careless spending, and as the noise rose and blood was shed, the Watch would come and the fighters would vanish away, save for the one or two unlucky ones who spent the night in the lock up.

The autumn changed from gold to brown, with clinging, damp November mist rising from the river, and slick streets, that were dark and treacherous. Francis knew his way a little now, studied as diligently as he was able and ventured out, hovering on the edge of groups of young men whose faces and names he recognised. He didn't understand why it was that Sidney Godolphin noticed him and singled Francis out to welcome and encourage him, introducing him to the eager crowd that stood around him. Unknown to him it was Sidney's instinctive, compassionate recognition, (sharp and unsettling as an unexpected sighting in a mirror), of Francis' bewildered entry, half boy, half man, into a world of buffeting noise and laughter that made no room for him. Small in stature, yet full of striking energy, humour and kindness, Godolphin was the centre of a group of clever, argumentative, affectionate young men. Young men who were in their last year at Oxford before leaving to join the Inns of Court, or a career in the diplomatic service, or the army, or take a seat in Parliament. King's men all of them, in their dress and manners, as well as in their allegiance, shown in their love of lace, the elegance of close-fitting satin doublet and sleeve, the curled hair and meticulously trimmed beards. Vanity, half-laughingly enjoyed, yet all of them prepared to answer the call to arms that would come within the next decade, and some would die in the Bishops' Wars, and many later in the long and bitter struggle of the Civil War. Perhaps the long shadow of a premature death, or the permanent unsettling of all once held to be certain and familiar, hung over them. The talk and laughter, the eager debate of ideas seemed, as Francis looked back long afterwards, to have been concentrated, brilliant, almost glaring in its intensity. They argued, explored, flung back and forth between them the political philosophy of Hobbes; the scientific ideas of Harvey regarding the circulation of the blood; the poetry of Donne, now going out of fashion but still delighting with both its erotic wit and the equally focused passion of his religious verse. Then, more heatedly, controversy regarding the Papist leanings of the queen, Henrietta Maria and her influence for good or ill at court; the right of the king to levy taxation, and my Lord of Buckingham's singular ineptitude at the siege of La Rochelle. Perhaps towards the end of such an evening, the mood would turn to the genial humour of the Devonshire clergyman, Herrick, whose poems circulated in manuscript among them, eagerly copied even though he had been a

Cambridge man. All, all of these things would weave their way into a conversation around the fire, flashing from one to another and Sidney catching the conversation and tossing it on, as though it were a ball made of scraps of leather, such as children play with. And around him, eager expressions, half mocking, half in earnest, and the evening ending with laughter or solemnity, and the bright faces going out into the night.

Long after, Francis remembered the radiance of such evenings. In later years, as the mood of the nation became sombre, and the divisions between the king's party and his opponents were no longer those of argument and intellect but of expressed contempt and hatred, it was vital to remember that there had once been wit, kindness, even companionship among men of differing opinions. Sometimes, Sidney would walk with him back to their rooms in college and invite him in for a glass of wine and show him a poem that he had written, or that he had in manuscript from another. He remembered especially one such night, late, long after midnight. The sharp stars overhead seemed to swirl as he gazed upwards, dizzy with the height of the towers around him. The quantity of ale that he had drunk and the exuberance of ideas caused him to stagger as he walked. But Sidney only laughed, not unkindly, and steered him towards the staircase and then to the settle in his room. He kicked the fading fire into sparks of life with his boot, and threw fresh logs on it, and brought out a bottle and glasses, but left them untouched. A knife of chill air slit the casement and set the candle flames wavering, to dip and dance. He turned to the chest, and brought out to Francis his treasured copy of the Folio, "Mr William Shakespeare's Comedies, Histories and Tragedies", five years old now, and handled with reverence. Francis studied the engraving of the playwright: a high dome of forehead, the pursed, enigmatic smile, eyes that looked over

Francis' shoulder and beyond; the stiff upright collar and doublet of another age. Theatre was almost unknown to him: plays and masques were performed most often in great men's houses and sometimes in the London theatres, but always there was the anxiety of plague and the disruption threatened by the growth of Puritan influence. He had only once stood at the back of a crowd and watched a play hang the vivid tapestry of words that, for brief hours had brought them into another room of life.

'Listen,' said Godolphin, taking the book from him. 'This is the season for it,' and began to read to him "The Winter's Tale". That night, and as they continued on other evenings, its slow unfolding story of friendship and the corrosive energy of jealousy, of loss and despair, and then its counterbalance of patience and redemption, took hold of him. 'Perhaps one day you will see it,' Sidney murmured, half to himself. 'Although it is not so much in favour now as other plays. But it is performed as a masque, and may have popularity at court. Who knows?'

Months passed, with greater contentment and confidence than he would have dreamed possible. But when Godolphin left to take up a seat in Parliament for Helston and then to travel abroad before being admitted to the Inns of Court, Francis lost touch with him. He had slowly made other friends at the university, and the growing confidence of his studies, and the work he did as a servitor in the Hall to supplement his meagre allowance, took all his time. When he thought of Sidney it was as a grateful remembrance of how he had been enabled to find his footing in a bustling and baffling world. He remembered his bright and cheering face, the smile of eyes and mouth, the ready encouragement and witty conversation, and scraps of poems read together, some of them Godolphin's own. He had copied one down, and went to find it from the chest that kept his few possessions from his student days, to read to Julia. They pondered it together, sensing both its generosity of spirit and its inherent sadness.

''T'is true that I could love no face
Inhabited by cold disdain,
Taking delight in others' pain.
Thy looks are full of native grace;
Since then by chance scorn there hath place,
'T'is to be hoped I may remove
This scorn one day, one day by Endless Love.'

After Sidney left Oxford, he and Francis did not meet again for almost four years, not until 1634.

***

Francis found it hard to describe to her, from the shared place of their present happiness, what it had been like for him to leave the university and move to London to work as a lawyer's clerk. Oxford had become for him a place of peace, of diligent study with the occasional reward of approval, of growing companionship and security, and even during the long summer holidays he had seldom gone home to Somerset. He knew he was not welcome: his father was soured by grief, by mounting debts, by the woeful failed pregnancies of his second wife, Madeline. Her greetings to him on his rare visits were kind but timid. Afraid lest his kindness should dissolve her careful composure, he guessed. He knew what she dreaded, daily: the shouts of bitter rage, the hurled platter across the table, the spilt ale or wine, the curses. Sometimes he would hear her low cries and smothered sobs after his father had staggered up to their bedchamber. He realised with a deepening sense of humiliation that he had fulfilled none of his father's hopes, neither in energy nor brilliance. And worse, his eyes and mouth echoed the picture of his mother that hung in the shadows of the hall: a haunting that could not be acknowledged; conceivably, a reproof. He would not return to live in the area, but must make his living elsewhere. And so, the lodestone of London drew him, equipped as he was with the university's preparation in rhetoric, dialectics and philosophy and his fluency in Latin, (less so in Greek, but enough), to seek out a training in the Inns of Court. A lawyer in Sherborne, who remembered his mother's family, wrote to recommend him. It was connection enough.

He sought poor lodgings in the winding lanes south of the River Thames. Rents were cheap and he had little to live on. There he struggled to study, to sleep, to find enough to eat, among the stews, bear pits and ale houses and the poor and tottering houses rented to the desperate. He rose early, under the sound of the bells of St Saviour, still remembered by the local people as St Mary Overie, to join the trampling muster of humanity with their carts and animals that thronged the roads from Kent to cross the river to the city. Francis learned to copy and then draw up articles of land sale and apprenticeships, wills and charitable legacies, trusts and grants and sworn testimonies. Sometimes he met with other young lawyers like himself, to drink and laugh and argue, and once or twice he went to the theatre, but they were in disfavour now as Puritan condemnation was vociferous and sometimes led to violence. And always there was the fear of disease: the swarming miasma of the plague in summer, the ague or the racking, blood-spittled cough of the fading sickness in winter that kept people from lingering at such gatherings. At night, tallow candles flared, guttering and stinking in gathering darkness. Once the restraining chill of winter passed, there was the strong fetid reek of the open drains that clogged the streets and the stink of the river itself as daylight warmed the city. Francis did not realise, until he struggled to describe it to Julia, how much he had hidden from himself his loathing of the town, his longing for the air and light of the country. His labour in the city was a necessity, and he was diligent. He could not see a release from it.

Yet he knew also that it held a perverse fascination for him. The vigour of its raucous cries and ceaseless movement, the fermenting ideas and gatherings around street preachers and ballad singers and broadsheet sellers, the murmuring discontent, the rumours of wars and news of fresh taxation. His lodgings south of the river took him amidst the poor, and there the restlessness thrived. The king in his palace of Whitehall became the object of their cursing, and with the king and his court, the lords of the Church, the bishops, and their resented wealth and their presentation of a God too remote, too magnificent to be approached by the poor. Where is the God of the poor? Where is the simplicity of the Gospel? Preachers, some of whom had paid for their so-called heresies with the ugly scars of cropped ears and the pale features of imprisonment, called for an end to idolatry and all its associations with the Bishop of Rome and their own queen. Some who gathered round them, nodding in passionate agreement, calling for purer worship and more just laws, won Francis' respect. He saw the devouring nature of taxation, the distance between subject and king, the hunger that men had for a religion that met their needs without robes and ritual. Yet he had found comfort in those same rituals, had experienced peace and order in the ceremonies of the church. His old priest had been a kindly and gentle man who led to God by example and never kept his people at a distance through fear or rank.

Francis' debates at university had confirmed in him the necessity of order, of change through process, of devotion to an allegiance once given. Each one of these elements was alive for him yet there was a tumult of ideas and passions, loyalties and divisions, and all the time as he listened, he could sense them gathering like the floods of his own Levels. Pray God there would be rhynes enough to take the tumult of waters when it came, as it surely must.

He returned, briefly, to his home in the summer of 1633. His father had been taken seriously ill, and he had been sent for, making the journey by cart and carriage as best he could over three days, and pausing in Sherborne only to hire a horse at the *George Inn* before riding the miles northwest of Yeovil to his home. He arrived, smothered in the dust of the lanes, and found his timid stepmother, Madeline, waiting for him. She whispered to him that his father was recovering, already well enough to come downstairs and demand of her and of the household that they meet his needs. Bring him food and drink, his clothes and riding boots, news of the farm. But she told Francis of the doctor's warnings: 'Any more of this rage and over-exertion and he could die of apoplexy,' he had stated firmly, shaking his head, though looking kindly at her. 'Too much rage and choler. Black bile and bitterness.' The doctor was old, and old-fashioned in his diagnoses. Yet sharp in the instincts of kindness he had developed in long years of accompanying his patients from birth and birthing to death and its fears and sorrows. But he was not afraid to tell the patient the truth of his condition, even though his words were met by twitching fingers that plucked the coverlet, starting eyes and the engorged face, purpled and mottled, that told of the truth of his condition. 'Walk more carefully,' the doctor had warned him. 'Carefully, lest you stumble and take a fall from which there will be no rising.' And for a time it seemed that his words were heeded. Francis was greeted with something like cordiality, the meal was served and eaten without episodes of fury and Madeline recaptured the ghost of the charm that had once graced her, years ago when his father had courted her.

'He has been gentler,' she said to Francis, her eyes begging him to forgive this man who had become so harsh a stranger to them both. 'He spoke of you, when he was very ill and weak. He wanted to see you.'

Francis lingered for several days and although he saw his father grow stronger, the hoped for conversation between them did not take place. He rode away, sad, regretful; troubled for his stepmother, aware that he could do nothing either to ease her situation or to win his father's affection.

'But it was on my way home that I first saw you,' he said to Julia, knowing her delight in the story, and remembering always how it had transformed him, even then, with a glimpse of innocence and happiness that he had not believed possible.

'I saw you,' he began, solemnly, prolonging the telling, teasing her. 'You were dancing in the street with your friends and your maid, to the tunes of a begging-fiddler.'

A bright morning in July. He had brought the horse back to the inn and paid the hire charge and booked a place on the coach that would creak its way on to Kington Magna and to Shaftesbury. There he might get the London coach or a bed for the night and the back of a cart for the next stage of the journey. He felt the overwhelming desire to postpone his return, to stay in this huge landscape of quiet, where rounded hills rose up from his own Levels to merge into the sky. Heights that had been shaped and scooped (men said) by ancient tribes who had made their homes, herded their sheep and cattle here and left these winding lanes and sinking ditches; lanes so deeply trodden now that the banks were higher than a man's head. Here, he thought, here is where I would choose to stay, where the haunches of the hills are like sleeping hounds, the tracks curving along their flanks. He was walking down Cheap Street, looking to find the turning for the abbey, when he saw her and stopped for the sheer joy of it. The jauntiness of the music, the innocence of the girls, hand in hand, turning to right and left, lilting and swaying to the tune, then breaking hands and clapping together to its rhythm. He half hid in the doorway, but one of them glimpsed him and they broke off, laughing, and scattered away. Only the maid, older perhaps and less shy, lingered a moment.

'Who is that?' he asked her, pointing.

'Julia, the glover's daughter,' she answered, smiling, and then overcome, she rushed to follow her mistress into the gateway and through the open door.

He could not explain the delight or the mystery of what he had seen. A glimpse of a candle in darkness, the freshness of air in a stale room, the breaking of buds at the onset of spring. He had turned to the fiddler, fumbling in his satchel for money to give him. A poor reward. He noticed the man's condition now. Ragged. The left leg crooked at an angle, and the clumsy crutch under the arm, all but disguised by the fiddle he held, silent, across his breast, no longer under his chin. The bow in his right hand, and the right hand missing two fingers. A lined and weary face: hard to believe that such radiance could come from his music.

'Thank you,' said Francis. 'You have suffered wounds, I think? In the army?' He gave him what he could afford and more.

The fiddler smiled, shrugged. 'The army. Under my Lord

Buckingham at La Rochelle.' He spat. 'No care for returning soldiers, wounded in his service. I play and beg. I live.'

'All the way home I thought of you,' he told Julia, laughing even now with the miracle of it. 'All the way home, and for ever after.'

***

Perhaps it would have remained a dream, a fragment of memory to smile about for a little time and then forget. But it cheered the heart to remember, he found, as summer hardened into autumn and the winter came to city streets and bitter cold gripped him every morning as he rose and shivered and ran from his lodgings to work. He would let his mind play with the dream: perhaps if he worked hard and gained the recommendation that he would need he could return to the West Country and set up as a lawyer, and find her and marry her. It gave some kind of purpose, however fantastical, to the struggle of each day. But it might inevitably have lapsed, he thought, and all this would have been lost, if he had not met Sidney one January day in 1634. He had been returning from an errand to deliver documents to one of the great houses along the Strand, and to witness a signature. Suddenly, amidst the restless throng of passersby, a voice, and a hand on his shoulder.

'Francis! Francis! Now this is a wonder!' The cordial, unforgettable voice of Sidney Godolphin.

That evening they met to eat and talk, long into the night. Godolphin had studied like himself, joining the Inns of Court before travelling widely. He had served in Parliament briefly in 1628 before an outraged Charles prorogued it in March 1629 for its intervention in matters that he saw as his Divine Right.

‘If only he had listened,’ Sidney said gravely, as an aside. ‘Taxation. Religion. We could have worked with him. Now I fear that the extremes of opinion will tear us apart. I see them hardening every day.’ But he was back in London, active in the king’s service at court, and likely to be sent abroad again on diplomatic business. He was disquieted, but his loyalty undisputed, as it would always be.

‘But come,’ he asked, turning the conversation away from the seriousness of his concerns. ‘Tell me of yourself.’ And Francis told him: his present studies and possible hopes of return one day to the West Country. He did not speak of the girl; already she was more vision than substance to him. Sidney could sense more than he was being told. He saw the underlying, dogged misery of a young man alienated both by the nature of the work and the environment in which he must live. He was not fitted for this tedium, or for the daily invasion of sense and privacy that was inescapable in London. Some men thrived on it, loving its vigour and variety, but not Francis. Over some men it cast a shadow, darkening their lives. ‘Come,’ he said. ‘You remember what we read together? “The Winter’s Tale”? It will be performed at the court two days from today, on the 16th January. Come as my guest. At last, you will see the performance.’

***

Entering with his friend, Francis found a world so different from his own that he felt he walked within the charmed circle of the play itself. Fashion and fragrance, courtliness and grace of bearing, the rustle of silks and satins, richness of colour, delicacy of lace. The paintings and hangings of the Banqueting Hall caught gleams of light. All seemed to be the costumes and scenery for a performance in which everyone, audience and actors alike, had a part. But the play itself, with all its dreamlike elements of masque and its compression of time, seemed to him to enact the terrifying consequences of unreasoning power and the vulnerability and torment of love. Yet still, waiting for a generation, and always uncertain, was the fragile yet triumphant work of reconciliation.

We are all players, he thought, *held captive within the dream of another,* and he looked around to see the king, aloof, calm, within whose imagination he felt they were conducting this slow and costly dance. He brought himself back to the play itself, withdrawing from what had become a maze of thought which he feared to enter.

The play had moved across the years as Florizel and Perdita took their delicate steps together. Francis forgot that Perdita was a boy of unbroken voice, in a wig and gown:

...when you do dance, I wish you
A wave o' the sea, that you might ever do
Nothing but that; move still, still so,
And own no other function.

He thought of her, Julia the glover's daughter, dancing to the music of a fiddler, and the words attached themselves to her and long after lingered in his mind like the swaying motion of the sea that they described and brought her vividly before him. *How old was she?* he wondered. *Fifteen, perhaps, sixteen? And I am all of twenty-two years old, without the means to marry. A profession to which I am indifferent; a stranger to my home.* Yet the words wove themselves into what had become a fading dream of her and brought it sharply back to him, with painful longing. "*I do wish you a wave of the sea... move still, still so.*" It gave him purpose, suddenly. To return to Sherborne, to meet her, to ask for her hand, to work now with perseverance to be able to marry her. Even if the waiting was nigh unbearable, he would wait and work for that.

'And you found me,' she said, simply, resting against his shoulder as they lay in the great bed one night. 'You came for me.'

Chapter Five

Francis

He had returned and found her.

A long and bitter winter and a reluctant spring had followed his meeting with Sidney. But as the uncertainties of April gave way to a calm and warm May and the roads dried and cleared, he took leave, long overdue, from his legal masters and began his journey west to Shaftesbury. Three days later he paid a few pence to a carter so he might sit on the back of the cart through the trundling lanes nearer to Sherborne. The rest of the way he walked, glad of the activity, glad of the chance to see again primrose under hedge and the reclusive violet, to breathe an air so wide that it banished London from his nostrils and cleansed its lingering taint from his clothes. Glad, too, to calm his mind that raced with the excitement of his hopes yet stumbled with the fear that this was all a folly. A dream of no substance.

He ought, he knew, to visit his father and stepmother, and must do so. There had been no news of them and he felt sure that somehow news of his father's health would have been sent to him even through the sullen mud and rain of winter, if there had been need for him to return. But he must go now, and that distracted him, troubled as he was with the uncertainty of how to find and speak with her. Julia, the glover's daughter. And more importantly, with her father and her mother. How would they receive him? A law student with no practice in sight, the poor relation of a declining family. He did not know, and yet the desire in him, the compelling dream, drove him in the face of all that could be thought reasonable.'"*The lunatic, the lover and the poet*,"' he said to himself, remembering evenings reading with Sidney. Then, wryly, '*and who knows which of the first two I am?*' His laughter lifted him and so he turned towards the town.

Above him rose the huge defensive walls and earthworks of the castle and the northeast gateway, and Walter Raleigh's crumbling dreams of splendour lay within. A mansion of light and wealth, unfinished, cruelly abandoned, its owner imprisoned in the Tower for thirteen years before a last and fruitless dream brought him to the block, when Francis had been a child of four years old. News of it had disturbed the West Country: old loyalties of seamanship and exploration and comradeship ran deep there. Francis shook from himself the sense of foreboding, a fear of the doom of dreams and dreamers. He entered the town, remembering well his years of schooling here. He knew and loved the golden honey stone of its walls. He saw again in his mind the intricate tracery of fan vaulting in the abbey church where a boy might lose himself gazing upwards in the quiet dusk of winter afternoons. And so, walking with no plan of what he would do or say, he came along Long Street and turned right into Cheap Street. He knew her house, even her name.

Perhaps, he thought, though he was not one to seek the invocation of the saints, so he was half-laughing, self-mocking as he did so. *Perhaps there is a kind saint who intercedes for lunatics and lovers.*

Before the ancient Hospice of St Julian, he remembered, and on the left. An arched gateway. A small enclosed garden. A half timbered building of some prosperity, but not so much that it would place her unattainably above him he hoped. He stood, hesitating, at the gate. Then, as he turned to look back down the street, he saw her, coming towards him, walking with her maid. They had been to market and in her hand was a laden basket. He stepped towards her down the street, and said words of such seeming-foolish formality that they laughed at them together ever afterwards.

'Mistress, may I help you with your basket?'

It had been so easy. She looked at him and smiled and she was as he remembered, even as he had dreamed. A lightness and grace in all her movements. Brown eyes, head slightly tilted as if to get the measure of him. Brown curling hair that escaped her cap. Her maid took care to examine him more closely, but something about him seemed both safe and familiar.

'I saw you,' he said, hesitantly. 'Once. And long ago. You were dancing with your friends to the tune of a begging-fiddler.'

Around them in the street all was hushed. The grind of wheels and steady clip of hooves, the cries and calls of children, the excited barking of a dog, faded from their hearing just as the street itself with all its busyness and buildings seemed to step back to leave them in this little pool of space and time. He could never remember what he said to her, only that she did not laugh at him, and that later that day he was calling nervous, but determined, to ask her father whether he might have his permission to court his daughter.

Edward Richard Glover, merchant, was prosperous, but not so much that he would despise even distant alliance to the

Phelips family. He was old now, for Julia had been the happy gift of his second marriage. His face was kind; a little weary, with a net of lines at the corner of his eyes and furrows gathered vertically above the bridge of his nose. His thumbs, double-jointed, flexed constantly as though testing the texture of the air as he would leather or cloth.

'My daughter's hand in marriage, eh?' he said, but not unkindly, looking with interest at the young man in front of him. Shabby but well-brushed clothes; too thin, he thought as he regarded him, and he noted the eyes that winced with uncertainty. A good broad mouth but unpractised in laughter. A lined face: too much study, too many books. Old before his time.

'How old are you, young man?' he asked, and if his voice seemed gruffly formal it was because he loved his daughter and wished her to be happy and safe in a world that even in Sherborne, seemed to be trembling with uncertainties.

'I am twenty-two, sir,' answered Francis, and he could see already the questions shaping themselves behind the merchant's eyes. How will you provide for her? What prospects can you offer her? And he began to fit his reply to the unspoken enquiries and sought to find words to convince her father of his determination to qualify for the law and seek a practice here in Somerset so that she might not lose her closeness to her family. 'And I will work and wait, sir,' he said. 'Until I can provide for her and give her a home.'

But Edward Glover's question came unexpectedly. 'Can you make her happy?' he asked abruptly. 'Little else matters to me. She was born of happiness, late in life for me, and my dear wife died three years ago. Julia has given me happiness even in the grief we have shared, and I will not give her hand to any man who cannot bring her joy.' His eyes scrutinised Francis for many heart beats of time. Then he nodded as if the fabric of the man had been felt and tested.

'I have very little to give her as a dowry,' he added. 'My sons have all my inheritance. They are in business of their own now, in London, chasing the fashions of the age in gloves and all manner of leather fineries.' He smiled, wryly. 'They did not like my second marriage, and in all these past sixteen years they have seldom visited. Julia is almost a stranger to them.'

When Francis left the house, late that afternoon, he saw Julia again, just briefly, in the garden to the left of the house. 'Will you wait for me?' he asked. 'I must study to set up as a lawyer first and make a home for you.' He stammered with the uncertainty of what lay ahead. 'It may - it will be years. Will you wait?'

And she, seeing him as though she had always known him, had always waited for his coming, with all the wisdom of the years spent loving her father and enduring with him through grief and loss, answered simply, 'Yes.'

'I will write to you,' he said, turning as he walked away down Cheap Street, and turning many times more to glimpse her as she stood at the gate.

The next day he rode over to see his father and stepmother. This was not news to share with them, not until he had found his independence and could outface the likely coldness of his father's response. He found them much as he had left them in the summer. His father was grey and thinner now, with empty flesh that sagged at his neck and pleated in his cheeks. Minute threads of red had broken through on his nose, his cheeks, to give a livid colouring to his face. He was cold, dispassionate, seemingly forgetful of the cordiality of the last visit. A sullen resentment of the imminence of death; a refusal to take pride in his son. Bitterness had given him the grist of life to chew on, but there was little else.

'I suppose you have overspent your allowance, Francis.' A statement, not a question.

'No, sir,' his son answered. 'I live frugally, and work hard. I have managed on the allowance that you give me, and I thank you.' He saw his stepmother shift uncomfortably and felt a rush of pity for her. Surely she should be able to share in the happiness that he was feeling? Was there once for her, and even for his father, this sense of the dazzle of inner light, the dance of spirit that he now felt? He sought her out later that day, not to share his secret, but to satisfy himself that she was safe and well and not worn down by his father's demands and cold, repetitive unkindness. He could see that the passion of his father's rage had gone, but cruelty does not need passion to make itself felt. Quiet contempt would be enough. He found her in the herb garden, plucking marjoram and thyme, rubbing them between her fingers and cupping her hands to inhale their scent, to find maybe a moment's astringent joy in their fragrance.

'He is calmer now,' she said in response to his unasked question, answering instead the carefulness of his eyes, the sadness and anxiety that she sensed he felt. 'I do not know how long he will live. The doctor warns him against undue strain, and the farm goes to ruin. Its furthest fields are neglected. The hedges are overgrown, and the rhynes clogged with mud and unchecked weed and rush. He is too proud to ask help from you, and the farm hands know that he cannot ride out and so little or nothing is done to mend the estate. He will not listen to me.' She paused. 'I loved him once, you know,' she acknowledged suddenly to Francis, her eyes spilling tears. 'He was kind and generous at the beginning. But when we married, and I bore him nothing but stillborn babies or babes that only lived an hour or so, he turned from me. And all his anger, all his rage broke out at me. And at God, who took his first wife and left him, he said, nothing but straw and no harvest.'

Francis was distressed for her. To live in this place of sourness and ruin, her own griefs of barrenness despised and ignored. They stood together quietly as she struggled to master her tears, and he saw how she had aged, her hair grey at the temples and forehead where it showed beneath her cap, her face lined and pale.

'When he dies,' he found himself saying, 'trust me. I will make sure that you are provided for. Send for me if things should take a turn for the worse, and I will come.'

He embraced and kissed her, waiting for her last shuddering sobs to stop and for her to regain her composure. Then he left her in the garden, re-entering the house to say a brief, formal farewell to his father before he rode through the lanes before sunset to his bed at the *George Inn.*

***

Francis travelled back to London to take up the labour of his studies and his work: tedious and cross-cut against the very grain of his being, but now purposeful and enlivened by the promise of marriage. However long it would take to work, to earn, to qualify. Then to become a lawyer with a solid practice in Sherborne or a neighbouring town, and thus provide a home and a future for her: it was a vivid dream, real enough to keep him attentive and careful even through the long hot days of summer.

These were the close, oppressive days that brought the fear of plague. Plague was spread, men and women feared, by the thickening reek of the runnels that slithered down the streets, the pall of corruption that rose from the Thames as its waters were churned by the swift boatmen.

In August, Francis went down to Sherborne to visit Julia and her father, staying at the *George Inn* again. Then he hired a horse and rode to spend a day with his own soured father, grateful in that chill house for the welcome of his stepmother. He saw with growing compassion the wasting of his father's life, and the extraordinary kindness of his stepmother's care that did not falter, despite all indifference, despite the bitter ingratitude with which it was received. Then to London to await the long autumn, the streets chilling as the sun declined, and the onset of the shivering fogs and damp of November.

Working long hours in chambers, he became aware of the tensions that were growing between himself and others among the young lawyers. Disagreements that only a year or so ago would have been argued out with fervour but without enmity, had soured, then turned poisonous with venom. Men who had once been companions, sharing a drink together, complaining of the work, struggling in the winter to stay warm, in summer to work in sweltering heat and stench, now held each other at a distance, cursed one another, knew in a darkening part of themselves that they had become adversaries. The days passed, grouped themselves into weeks, then months, relieved only by the delight of her letters arriving and the time spent by guttering tallow candles writing to her. And each day, he told himself, brought him nearer to her. But it seemed interminable. The year ended and 1635 began, and all around him Francis sensed the slow stirring of discontent like a dangerous animal that is emerging from long hibernation. Murmurings against taxation, against religious practice. Against the king and his long-dissolved Parliament. Against the king's Papist wife and her influence. And, increasingly, support gathered for the compelling preaching of the Puritans: street crowds, some violent in opposition, some passionate in support. Stirrings too in Scotland, where church goers were alienated by the vestments and rituals enjoined by Archbishop Laud. London buzzed with news and rumour, virulent and bigoted on all sides, waiting, waiting, for ignition. For the flintlock spark to fall. So the year passed, and the next began.

Winter, with the roads closed to the countryside for all but the most urgent of journeys, imprisoned Francis in London. The streets were slimed with mud and waste. Sleet and snow and an east wind found out the numberless cracks in his cheap lodging house, and slit through the thinness of his garments. The air was thick and foul from coal fire smoke that clung to the roofs, clogging the streets and alleys with fog. It covered London as a pall, seen from the surrounding hills as a brown thickening of the sky, through which pricked the spires of churches. Francis was ill that February, coughing and shivering and alone. Each day he struggled to get to the Inns of Court to work, half-blind with the exhaustion of fever as he crouched over the documents he copied, and stumbling as he took them for signature to my Lord's house in Westminster, along the chill riverside. Hurrying back against the easterly wind, late one February day, he did not recognise Sidney, meeting him by a seeming miracle, but Sidney saw him and taking hold of his shoulder, seized him with the roughness of urgent compassion, and brought him to a neighbouring tavern. Harsh wine first, grating his throat, and the fire's heat, excruciating to his stiff and numbed hands. Then food.

'Slowly, slowly,' said Sidney as Francis tried to mop up the stewed meat with the bread and swallow it too hastily. Shamed and desperate, Francis found he was crying as he looked at him and he struggled to thank him, through a mouth too thickened with food and tears and cold to shape his words. And Sidney waited, drinking his wine alongside, smiling with uncomplicated kindness and unchanged it seemed to Francis in those initial blurred moments, since they had last met. Indeed, unchanged since their student days all those years ago.

Later, as the wine, food and fire did their work of restoration, Francis looked at his friend more carefully and saw clearly now that time and anxiety had aged him. There was a certain grimness about the set of his mouth, and his forehead was creased with fine lines. The eyes, still full of life and kindness, were nonetheless puckered in the corners. Sidney, far more than Francis, could see where events were leading. He saw a king, blindly unaware of the mounting volume of discontent. Cocooned within the Palace of Whitehall, his majesty remained detached and remote from the stirrings of opposition that had found a multitudinous voice in street preaching and broadsheets and in the sullen mutterings of taverns and street corners; in the growing defiance of the king's taxation measures, foreign policy and religious tendencies. Sidney would never cease to be the king's man, and to give his support to those whom King Charles appointed, but he knew the precariousness of the old order and saw with dread the inevitable collision of past and future. Before Francis would meet him again, he would be away with the king's army to fight in the mismanaged, humiliating Bishops' Wars between the king's forces and the far more effective Scots.

But on that day of meeting the confrontation of war, in all its hideous and disastrous manifestations, was still to come. Yet Sidney Godolphin sensed its coming as a farmer might sense the gathering of a storm on the edge of the horizon and look with dread on his unharvested fields. This time of encounter with Francis, these hours of comradeship and reminiscence, were a brief respite for him from the strain of political reality. He would return from them to the court and to the perilous refinement of his royal master: the magnificent collection of paintings, the patronage of the arts, the elegance of fashion and manners, the dangerously overt Catholic sympathies of the king's adored wife, Henrietta Maria. A costly loyalty, but founded in a profound belief in the right and ordained order of things, the essential "degree" that holds a society together. Honour, vows taken, would hold him to this loyalty always.

'Tell me of yourself,' Sidney urged, noting that colour had returned to Francis' face and that he had eased back into the bench before the fire. 'Tell me what has happened to you since we last met.' So, with encouragement, Francis told his story. Making light of the long hours of study, the harsh conditions of his lodgings and financial stringencies, he told of what enabled him to continue. A girl dancing, glimpsed in a Sherborne street, the dream of her that sustained him as he worked to achieve some kind of financial security. The willingness to wait; her father's agreement. Even the coincidence of the play when he had last seen Sidney and the lingering words that had caught her image and given it substance. All this he recounted, hesitantly, and Sidney encouraged him when the words ran dry.

'So, Julia,' said Sidney. He smiled and, teasing him a little, quoted from Parson Herrick, so popular when they had been together at Oxford.

'"*When as in silks my Julia goes,*
Then, then, methinks, how sweetly flows
That liquefaction of her clothes."'

But looking at Francis' stricken face, he realised that this was not a thing for even the kindest laughter. 'No, I was wrong,' he said. 'This is true for you.' He looked at him with a kind of wonder. Envy perhaps. 'Not a thing for laughter.' Then, so gravely aware of the undercurrents of what was already gathering and would, he knew with terrible presentiment, be happening in the months and years ahead, he spoke again, and reminded his friend of another of Herrick's lyrics. '"While you may, go marry",' he said half seriously, half jokingly. And then again. 'No, this is not for laughter. Go marry, Francis. As soon as it is possible for you. Seize the happiness that is offered.'

Francis returned to his lodgings in fresh heart. Warmed, fed, heard. As the slow and dismal days of February moved into March, the air quickened and revived, even in the sombre streets, and the hope of April stirred. In walled gardens, blackbirds sang and there were glimpses of blossom. Soon he might claim leave and travel west, to call on her and inevitably also, as duty required, visit his father and stepmother.

When, in the years that followed, he would tell Julia, to her endless delight, the stories of finding and dreaming, and speak of his friend Godolphin and how salvaging that day had been for him, he would also wonder how they had endured such delay, such distance. Yet it was so, imposed upon them for two more years before he could marry her and before they could begin their lives together. The years passed with the rhythm of the seasons: a strange regulator to a man whose life was lived within the confines of the city. In winter, from late October to early April, the roads were almost impassable and he could not travel. Spring and summer brought meetings and certainty and love that deepened with waiting and faithfulness.

Sometimes he talked with her and with her father about the growing discontent, the seething disquiet of the city. At street corners, compulsive preachers would grip a restless audience, men, women, children snatched out of a crowd to listen to their rhetoric: the vehement denunciations of Popery and the ceremonial of Archbishop Laud's impositions. A theology of judgement and the terror of hell, of the salvation of the Elect, the certain damnation of all who worshipped idols and images. Some had suffered for their faith: cropped ears, branded cheeks. Their passion and sincerity moved him. Others spoke similar words but from a different heart, and he saw how they stirred and compelled a different spirit. Violence, cruelty, hatred, sprang up like tares in the wheat. He watched a group of boys, perhaps no more than twelve or thirteen years old, young boys at the start of their apprenticeships, who strained like hounds with the excitement of the words, the promises of powers yet to come. And all supported with a mangled text: "Daughter of Babylon, doomed to destruction; happy is he be that takes and dashes your infants against the stones". So easy then to move to the fluent insults and abuse and to the watchwords: "Beware of the Whore of Babylon; the idolatry of Rome; the Jezebel". So easy to give those impulses to violence a vindication and a cause. Francis, seeing the rapt faces, the maleficent vision, shuddered with the dread of what might be unleashed.

The seasons turned and his work was less arduous now as he grew familiar with its language and tenets, practice and precedents. In winter, he made his way daily through the sludge of the streets along Fleet Street to the Inns of Court; as spring quickened in the air, he took leave to travel down to Sherborne, enduring the jolting carriages, the frequent halts in quagmires of mud, to arrive at Shaftesbury to find a friendly carter, or to walk the lanes, and every moment nearer to her, and to his hopes. Summer in London, with its stink of effluent and offal on hot days; the Thames, stirred by the boatman's oars, gurgling with its secret thickened lading of clogged water, that quickened to the rush and race of the one bridge: these things became part of him, familiar and now endurable. In the summer of 1636 he escaped the overcrowded and fetid slums of Southwark, returning in the autumn to find a city in mourning, a charnel city of thousands dead of the plague. Horror and pity filled him. Yet there were some, hoarse with their vision of righteousness, who turned such suffering into the judgement of God.

But that summer, and the spring of the next year, set him free, to travel more easily, to stay longer. A familiar and welcome visitor, no longer staying at the *George Inn,* but at her home.

In May 1637 he was summoned back to Somerset. A sudden summons, hammering on the door of his lodging late in the evening. An ostler from the nearby inn, a note in his wallet. "My dear son Francis," his stepmother had written. Laborious letters on the yellow-white paper. "I beg that you come quickly. Your father has not long to live."

He slept little, rising to catch the first coach out of the inn yard, travelling slowly through the villages of Clapham and Merton, Esher and beyond, to the road that lay west, still bright with overnight puddles that caught the glint of the early sun. All along the hedgerows, he sensed the stirring of birds and saw the hawthorn budding and breaking. He felt a terrible impatience with the steady trot of the horses, the delays when the team were changed, the inevitable grounding in mires and ruts not yet dried by a summer sun. Three days and they were at Shaftesbury, then on to the road for Sherborne: a walk through lanes, a ride on a cart part of the way and then the chance meeting with another labourer, one of his father's old hands, who set him beside him as he drove his cart along tracks that wound northwest to circle Yeovil and that brought him at last to the house.

He entered and his stepmother came running. There were no words needed now, and she took his hand and led him to the bedchamber where the man who had once seemed so tall and stern and powerful lay hollowed and frail under the covers. Curiously diminished, breathing in gasps, only the dull eyes moved to show that he was waiting for him as his son came in the door. Francis stood watching, delving within himself for the words, the feelings that were appropriate for this time, this unique time. His father's hands plucked impotently at the sheets and Francis realised that he was seeking for his hand, to hold it. He drew nearer, closer than he had ever been in his memory, to this man he called father. Perhaps as a little child? He did not know. He had no recollection of tenderness. He touched and held the hand that had groped restlessly towards him. Tears smarted in his eyes.

'Father,' he said hesitantly. 'I came as swiftly as I could.'

But the man who lay stretched and gaunt before him was not listening. His breaths quickened as he struggled to speak. 'I wronged you,' he muttered, clumsily framing the words through the paralysis that had taken part of his face. He stirred again. 'I wronged you, Francis. Too like your mother. It could not be borne.' He lapsed then and Madeline came forward to draw Francis away.

'He will rest now,' she said gently. 'Later, perhaps, he will speak again.'

Francis looked down. The shrunken lids had fallen on the eyes. The cheeks, collapsed in scrumpled folds of flesh were crackled with fine red lines, like the glaze on an earthenware pot. The tortured breathing eased and became more even, though shallow and rasping. 'I will sit with him,' he told his stepmother. Then spoke quietly to her, 'Have you sent for a priest?'

'The old parson has gone,' she told him, simply. 'A new priest, no,' she corrected herself. 'He cannot be called that. A new vicar, Ezekiel Cropper, has come. A man of new ways, and we struggle to follow them. I will send for him, but your father may not allow him near him.'

Francis sat beside his father all that day and far into the evening. The old man breathed hoarsely, sometimes opening his slack eyes to search for Francis but there were no more words. Rage had filled and fleshed his father like air in a pig's bladder: now it was running out, draining away in a sigh of immeasurable regret.

They were lighting the candles as the sun dipped beyond the line of willows at the edge of the far field when the parson came. He stood beside the bed, a pale, attenuated man, sombre in dress and manner, ruthlessly conscientious. He brought judgement into the room and his words stirred the dying man to stumbling, indistinguishable words. Only the enraged resentment of the eyes spoke for him as the parson read to him from the sternest of Psalms. Francis drew away as his father was urged to remember his sinfulness and the awfulness of judgement. For a few hours he had seen a man he thought implacable melted into something near to gentleness, whose truth must now be known to God. This harsh righteousness could bring no comfort.

'I think, sir,' he began, touching the vicar on the arm and drawing him away. 'I think my father needs to sleep and he can no longer hear and respond. I thank you for your coming, and your prayers.' He led him downstairs. If there were moments of life left, they did not belong to this man, but to his stepmother, and to himself, and if there were repentance needed it would not come at the command of this austere minister. He waited courteously as the parson mounted his horse, brought round from the stable by John, his father's one remaining manservant, and watched him ride away. Aloof and silent, this new parson, but with a smouldering passion for his truth. The days of the old priest who drew his flock by gentle means into the Kingdom of Heaven and rarely spoke in anger except to challenge cruelty; those days were gone. Francis recognised the same spirit as he had heard in street preachers in Southwark: undeniable sincerity, yet a pitiless disregard for human frailty.

That night, just as the darkest hours moved slowly towards a grey dawn of birdsong, his father slipped beyond them both as they sat at his bedside. Just for a moment, his father's eyes had rested on Madeline and softened. She wept at his departure. Slow heartbeats later they rose up, stiff and cold, to renew the candles, and in the early hours of the morning, Madeline and Marjory, John's wife, washed the body and dressed it in a linen shroud. Beneath the stuffed bolster of the bed, where it had lain throughout his illness, they found a miniature. A woman whose face Francis could barely remember, whose death had robbed him of a mother, and her husband of life itself and had left him only a husk; a cold, angry stranger.

When they had buried him, next to his long dead wife at last, Francis searched for the papers that might tell him of the household affairs. His father's debts and negligence had robbed the estate of all its assets. Neglect had diminished it to a farm of few and unproductive cattle, fields that had not been ploughed or cultivated for several years, barns near collapse. Hedge and ditch had been left unattended and overgrown. His father's men had been turned off one by one as the work dwindled. There was little left, save perhaps one small house at the edge of what had once been a thriving property and the few fields that surrounded it. His first and grateful concern was for his stepmother. She must be provided for and if she chose to return to her relatives in Muchelney, she should not go without resources to sustain her with dignity in widowhood. Most of the farm would be sold off. Its dilapidated buildings and wasted land must go to some more prosperous local farmer or distant member of the family, to be revived, and almost all that could be made of such a sale should go to her.

Francis set himself to sell the property to ensure Madeline's well-being, and to see whether out of all that had been brought to ruin he could salvage the small farm that had been built more than fifty years ago on a crest above the level fields. He knew without doubt that his days in London were over. A small farm. His future lay in the restoration of the house and buildings, however decaying, and the abandoned land that gathered round it. John and Marjory and their daughter Nell might come with him if he asked, and that would be sufficient. There would be enough, if he worked hard, to make a home for Julia. Enough to live on. If he laboured through the summer months and broke up the land for the spring sowing and could somehow eke out what little had been made from the sale to buy just a few cows and sheep, perhaps he might ask for her hand, and in the summer of next year, bring her home as his wife.

Chapter Six

Francis, Julia

'Love is enough,' she always remembered saying, as he carried her into their home. Perhaps they were the words she took with her into the dark.

***

But darkness was unimaginable in that day of homecoming as he carried her into their home and swept her from window to window to look out over their home, their land. A true homecoming, one they had both been waiting for all their lives, and its rich content satisfied them even beyond the joy and discoveries of passion. Marrying in the abbey church in Sherborne, with few witnesses, but with her father's love to bless them and Madeline's ungrudging delight, Francis and Julia made vows that hardly needed words before they travelled through the slow green lanes to reach the house just before the sun touched the horizon. In the weeks and months that followed they worked together, he in the fields, she in the house and garden, to build the farm again.

Gradually the land yielded to the plough and broke open to

rain and seed. Over the months, John worked steadily alongside Francis to care for the stock and he taught him how to plough the small field beyond the orchard. The two cows and the small flock of sheep grazed in the nearby fields and they had filled the barn with midsummer hay to be winter fodder for them. Together with their neighbours, they cleared the rhynes of debris, unclogging the channels that had narrowed with mud and broken branches, ensuring that they would run free for this coming autumn's rains and leave a legacy of drained pasture for the future. In the evenings, Julia and Marjory heard Francis and John talking together about the sowing of wheat in the New Year and the slow, steady cycle of the following seasons. Francis, listening, questioning sometimes, and learning constantly from the measured wisdom of the older man. At harvest time, John told him, men from the village will come with their scythes, just as he and Francis would in turn help them, and after winnowing, the straw gathered in the barn must serve them for the winter. The winnowed wheat was to be ground into flour at the mill in the village, and the straw would be bedding for the beasts.

Marjory's young daughter Nell took charge of the hens, shooing them out from under her feet whenever she walked across the small yard. Greedy for scraps, they would gather to her whenever they heard her voice. The house grew alive round them with furniture, much given by her father, and with tapestries and covers, some the work of her mother's hands, some that Julia embroidered. Marjory cooked and kept the house with her; the dairy and larder and the sweeping and cleaning a shared pleasure between them. The two women were close and it was to Marjory that Julia confided her hope, trusting in the older woman's experience and kindness.

'We will have a baby, Francis. Our baby,' she whispered to

him one night, drawing his hand to feel beneath her heart. And all night they lay close, stirring to talk and sleep and wake again, she encircled by him, his arms holding close this beloved wife, this beloved child.

It was late spring, May, soon to become June. Warmth expanded to fill the skies and the fields, drying the soil, and bringing willow trees and bushes into bright leaf. The field edges and hedgerows were vital with flowers, white and cream, yellow and purple, and with birdsong and chatter. The rhynes glowed with the gold of Kingcups, reflecting back the amazement of the sun. Skylarks rose to weave the sky with song and the green-backed lapwing swooped and flocked to settle in the fields. Julia spent much of her time in the garden and in the small apple orchard that Francis had planted for her at the back of the house. Slowly the careful beds took shape as she had planned and she saw the beginnings of what, next year, would be her garden. Francis paid for the local mason to carve the joined initials "J" and "F" and "P" on the Ham stone lintel of the door, and the date of their marriage last year, June 1638. Stone, the mason told them as he worked, from the old Muchelney Abbey, taken away for buildings and repairs after the King Henry's commissioners had driven away the monks and seized their land, a hundred years ago. He showed them where, hidden from sight in the corner, the monks had carved a vine and grapes, now blurred with time and weathering.

Julia's father would often ride out to them in the fine weather. Welcomed and loved by Francis as well as Julia, he found great contentment in their home. His own sons, successful and wealthy merchants in London, rarely visited and when they did, they came alone, stiff and unyielding. He sensed that in their pursuit of wealth they had abandoned old ties, old ways. He had never seen their wives or his grandchildren. Greeted with delight as he was, after his long ride, he could not help but bring into their home news that Francis had hoped to forget, news that penetrated and jarred their enclosed world. News that had travelled slowly from London to Sherborne, but its shuddering urgency and disturbance could nevertheless be felt, and the protracted gathering of the tension between a king and his people was palpable.

As the months of 1639 turned towards autumn, news came of the humiliation of the king's army in Scotland and of a seething discontent that would result in the recall of Parliament. Francis did not know that his friend Sidney would ride north, struggling to change the outcome of what would be mockingly called "The Bishops' Wars" by the example of his own personal gallantry. The diseases of the nation, religious, economic, constitutional, were clustering like ulcers on the body of the state.

But Francis and Julia, so strong in their personal happiness, believed that in some miraculous way their sanctuary of life would be inviolate, pitting their love and trust in one another against the numberless and nameless fears of the future. Their chief disquiet now was that the church where they worshipped was being stripped of ornament and altar rail. Its austerity made them feel like strangers. Men, whose faces Francis remembered from childhood, shouted now for the dismemberment of the chancel, with voices hoarse with zeal, their wives also and children, shrill in their approval. The statues of ancient and forgotten saints were dislodged and broken to become rubble for walls or foundations, or the mending of gaping holes in roads. Religious tensions had become local as well as national. After the old parson's death, some had welcomed the zealous Ezekiel Cropper, who brought with him the fundamentalism of the Puritans, demanding simplicity of altar and liturgy. With his own hands he had begun removing carvings and statues and some joined him, the destruction and damage releasing a kind of frenzied pleasure among its participants, a self-gratification oddly at variance with the austerity and rigidity that he preached.

One Sunday, after the service, Francis found the statue of the Virgin thrown into the rank growth of nettles where men relieved themselves behind the church. Her praying hands were broken, her tender, vague face smeared with mud or worse. He felt such a shaking of outrage and disgust that he had no words to tell Julia what he had seen. For hours that afternoon he walked the fields, remembering the vehemence of street preachers, the clangourous incitement to hatred. The remembrance of London's streets lodged again in his nostrils and in his ears, together with an inchoate dread of imminent upheaval.

Autumn sank into winter and the rains came, grey and relentless, turning the highways to quagmires, the lanes to torrents of grey-brown water that rushed between their tall hedges and banks. The rhynes brimmed with darkly ominous water. Julia's baby was due just before Christmas: they hoped for the rain to ease and the roads to be clear enough for the doctor to come if sent for. Francis was confident that John would wish to ride through any weather to get help for her, and he struggled to wait and trust, to wait and trust, whilst knowing that despite his will, his mind was hauling submerged memories out of some dark and silent well of his own childhood remembrance.

In the chill hours of one morning of late November, long before the faint signs of grey daybreak had stirred in the skies, she gave a cry and he woke, instantly. Outside he could hear the battering of the rain and knew that the roads were impassably flooded. He struck flint and steel to light a candle and reached for his clothes, fumbling in his haste, and even in the midst of her pains, she smiled at him.

'Francis, Francis, get Marjory. All will be well. Get Marjory.'

Through the next hours, as Marjory tended her, and Nell busied herself with hot water and linen cloths and carefully folded and refolded the embroidered garments all three women had made so lovingly for this baby, he paced up and down in the house, feeling it to be too small for the desperate length of stride he needed to take. As the day broke, he pulled on boots and outer garments and walked outside in the drenching rain, round her orchard and between the beds of her garden, praying, fearing, remembering a small boy waiting at the corner of the stairs as though seeing himself as he once had been. A small white face, dark hollowed eyes, and no-one who would tell him of the catastrophe that had overtaken his life.

'Please God, not that, not that,' he prayed. Again and again. John came alongside him with gruff wordless sympathy, and Francis remembered then that their daughter Nell had come to them late in life and long past all hoping. He knew then the strength of this man's companionship and drew upon it.

Towards noon, he heard a cry. Thin, wavering, but insistent. Francis thrust his head through the door long before Julia was cleaned and ready for him and met Marjory's broad back. Then she turned to give him a glimpse of the red puckered baby she held in her arms. It was their son.

'All is well,' she told him, reassuring him as she would a child. 'All is well.'

And from behind her, Julia's tired yet triumphant voice. 'Come soon, Francis. We have a son!'

As winter closed in on them now, sealing the countryside under a weight of snow after Christ-tide and Epiphany, Francis and Julia dwelt within the rounded world of their delight. Before the snow set in, John had taken the news to Julia's father, and he had struggled through the short hours of daylight, one misty and chill day, to visit them and see his grandson. Sitting with them briefly, to break bread and drink ale before his return to Sherborne, he had brought no news for them of the world beyond their neighbourhood, not even from his sons in London, save a carefully worded letter sent to him at Christmas that showed that they were actively supporting those who were drawing up the long roll of grievances against the king. The shadow of uncertainty touched them for a moment. Beyond this room lay waiting for them, and for the child, an unknown and troubled world.

But the shadow passed, and the boy was christened Richard, for his grandfather, and Sidney for Francis' friend and they took him to Parson Cropper on the Sunday after Christmas Day, Julia having dutifully attended for her Churching three days before. His grandfather and John stood as his godfathers, and Nell, much in awe and blushing with the solemnity of the responsibility, as his godmother.

It was a harsh winter: there was barely hay and straw enough for the beasts and they were forced to slaughter one of the sheep to exchange for smoked meat and flour. Almost all the chickens, except the best layers, were taken for the pot, and poor Nell, tender-hearted, grieved for them and the familiar sound of their chuckling content. They lived closely together, the baby kept warm and fed, the rest of the household staying with Julia and Francis so that there was only one fire to burn their precious fuel. At last the weather began to ease. Frost ferns vanished from the windows. The path from the door to the barn, kept free as much as possible from drifting snow, now browned and muddied as the thaw came. The men struggled out to see to the spring sowing; the animals were led from the outhouses, blinking in the light, to the highest pasture above the flooded fields. The world had turned to hope again.

***

In the spring of 1640, Francis and Julia and the men and women of the small hamlet near to them could have had no means of seeing or knowing how rapidly their lives were rushing towards war. Only Sidney Godolphin, far from them, was attuned to the gathering swell of argument and dissension in the capital. He had attended the Short Parliament in April, before it was precipitately dissolved by the king. There he heard and felt the obduracy of the opposition ranged against the implacable conviction of King Charles. He could not have foreseen then, but saw with horror in the ensuing year, the ruthlessness of those who called for the execution, first of the king's advisor Strafford, and then, unsatisfied, for that of Archbishop Laud. As Member for Helston, Godolphin attended when Parliament was recalled, recognising the desperation of the king, who struggled against his nature to make a conciliatory move. But Parliament showed, instead of submission, awareness of its almost limitless powers and intensified its demands. And in the background, like a surge overriding the voices of moderate men, the city of London and other cities of trade and influence were stirred to revolt. Men of zeal and conviction stepped into the space left by a king who vacillated yet who would not compromise. Civil disorder boiled on the streets, especially in London, and those who wished to ally themselves to a cause of violence could find opportunity to do so, many hiding under a veil of pious conviction. The London apprentices banded together with shouts of passion and fervour, an inundation of restless energy to be easily swayed to violence in defiance of the king and all his laws.

It needed no prescience to see the inevitable collision of two opposing forces. Steadfast in his allegiance always, despite recognising that the opportunity for reconciliation had been ignored, Godolphin spoke bravely of the impending disaster to the country before leaving Parliament to prepare to fight for his king. In March 1642 Parliament issued the Militia Ordinance, seizing the right to raise an army in defiance of the sovereign. In June, King Charles sent out the long-forgotten Commissions of Array to every county, calling on his loyal subjects to raise the county militias. And so the nation divided. Sidney, filled with foreboding, returned to his home town of Helston in Cornwall, to raise his followers and enlist with them as a simple trooper in the army in the West Country.

***

That summer, the news ran with swift feet, confused, alarmist, imperative; gathering men to the cause they espoused, splitting families and friends. Old allegiances: new visions. Old entitlements: newly articulated grievances. Old certainties: new and passionate certitudes. Rumour became imminent, urgent, and reached the small village where Francis and his neighbours had begun the harvest. Even there, men began to group themselves, gathering to the rightness of their cause, the devotion to a creed, or to the promise of adventure, the excitement of unproved manhood, the lure of violence. Some sought out Abel the Smith, after twilight, to forge for them pikes and short swords from sickle and pruning hooks. And from the poor cottages of outlying farms and the meanest dwellings of the village many came to hear the message of Ezekiel Cropper who spoke of a new kingdom. A kingdom without earthly rank and its injustices. The bare, unencumbered chancel of his church, with its direct access to the table, told them of a God who did not hold himself aloof from their poverty and ignorance. Moved beyond words, some would seek out the army of Parliament, to fight and die for such a vision of God and man.

Yet far away from the cities where the discord had multiplied and untouched by the news that even now ran like the wind in the grass among the villages near to his home, Richard was growing up. And his glad childhood was totally unaware of the conflict that would shape the nation for the next decade and beyond. Safe within the farmhouse and later in the confines of the garden, he was learning to smile and laugh and speak, to stumble and walk and play. He was an endless joy to his father and mother, to his grandfather and to his step-grandmother, Madeline, who came to visit whenever she could and held him with poignant delight. And however tired Francis was, and however grimed from his day in the fields, he would see his son reach out his arms to him, and stride forward to swing him up onto his shoulders. Sometimes such happiness, such blessing, seemed too full a cup for Julia to carry.

Francis, unwillingly, realised that even this happiness was only a fragile dream of safety. The rumours of war, the gathering of armies, reminded him too strongly of the riots and clangour of crowds in the city. He knew that the terrible energy he had seen there, once unleashed, would creep nearer to engulf even this ancient land of waterways and the steady timeless rhythms of the plough and the reaping sickle. And so, one day in early August, 1642, Francis responded, as he knew he must, to the King's Commission of Array, and went to Sherborne to join Sir Thomas Lunsford's army. He had no sense of unquestioning loyalty to a cause; rather, a steady determination to act as he believed was right, to hold to what he saw as the stable order of the nation against the chaos that might ensue. Traditional family loyalties; friendships at Oxford; all too recent memories of the disturbances of London streets; all of these elements drove him to enlist. And unspoken, yet felt in the very essence of his being, there was the instinct to protect a wife and son from the unknown perils of war. He had some experience of swordsmanship but not of fire-arms whilst at Oxford, and of military service in the Trained Bands both in Oxford and here in Somerset, but he knew himself to be unprepared for the realities of conflict, the smiting of sword on sword, wounds, hardship, death. He walked slowly around the garden with his wife, the child in his arms, pausing to stand for a few moments to talk with John, pointing to the fields now ready for the plough, where the harvest had been scythed and gathered, and to the calm grazing cattle and sheep. Then, unable to find further words, he moved away. After buckling his saddlebags onto his waiting horse, he turned, stiff in the leather buff-coat, to reach out to embrace his wife and lift and kiss his son, who had clasped his boots, excited, puzzled by this stern and strange father. Then Francis rode away, looking back many times with unfelt cheerfulness to wave at the little grouping of his wife and child and John, Marjory and Nell who stood to watch him leave until he was out of sight. And for long after.

The next weeks held great uncertainty for Francis. News passed swiftly among the men, not always accurate, and they could have little idea of the strategies that were recruiting and moving armies hundreds of miles away from them. The Royalist army in the Southwest was gathering slowly, with only some of the necessary equipment yet available, and there was essential training both for men and horses in the manoeuvres of war. Soldiers with experience on the continent or in the ill-fated Bishops' Wars could give some guidance in those early, fumbling days of training. Through the hours of daylight, Francis learned how to load and fire the flintlock pistols whilst holding his horse steady between his thighs; how to draw his sword and press forward shoulder to shoulder with others in the compelling thrust of a cavalry attack. How to swing his heavy sword to decapitate the stuffed straw bodies hoisted on poles and turn his horse with his knees to avoid the side swipe of others. To recognise commands, to respond, to obey without question. It was sometimes dreamlike in its motion, often distasteful to him, yet it must be done. His life at the farm, his wife and child, seemed far from him, and he would not wish them to be part of this world where men solemnly prepared for slaughter.

Then, in the uneasy time of waiting, disquieting news came from the north. Hull, with its vital armoury, had denied entry to the king. The navy was controlled by Parliament. King Charles had raised his standard at Nottingham on 22nd August but to little effect and then marched through Derby seeking recruits. Both armies grew in number and as water gathers and trembles before it spills, so the opposing forces were poised for conflict. It was not long before the distant uncertainties became near, and imminent. News reached Francis, overheard, whispered down the line, as men gathered for their supper of broth with bread to wipe it from the bowl, of a Royalist success at Marshall's Elm not many miles away. Relief was soon followed by unease as they heard of the reaction of Parliament:

a formidable army was moving west, under the leadership of the Earl of Bedford. In response, the Royalist commanders decided to garrison and defend the old castle of Sherborne.

Yet, in fields throughout the land, the harvest still needed to be gathered and barns filled, and the hot sun of August smote down on sweating men and women and horses, garnering for life whilst armies prepared for war. Quartered in the town, Francis was sometimes able to visit his father-in-law and take brief refuge there from the unreal but compelling business of preparation for war. Once, he was free to ride out to his home, and be welcomed by their delight and relief, but he knew when he returned to quarters that it had unsettled him, that the austere enterprise of war demanded his entirety of being.

Chapter Seven

Julia

During the long, cloudless hours of daylight, Julia could find contentment in the games played with her son, now two, running and chasing through the newly planted lines of apple trees, and out on the harvested field, with the stubble prickling their legs. Or picking brambles to boil with honey to make jam for the winter, to store on the cool shelf in the cellar. And Nell, Julia's maid, when maid was needed, helped her mother, Marjory, and milked the cows and cared for the hens, and looked after young Richard, scampering after him and spoiling him. And she not much more than a child herself.

But at night, as evening settled in and Richard had been told his story and had his toes counted and they had played the tickling games that had them both hiding and laughing over and under the coverlets of the big bed, then, after she had settled him to sleep, Julia knew that she could not keep at bay any longer her fears for Francis and the slow dull ache of missing him. Sometimes she wrote to him, laboriously forming the shapes as her father had taught her long ago, uncertain how to send the letters, or whether he would ever receive them, but needing to write to him anyway. "O my dear love, I pray each day that you come home to us safe and soon," she wrote. Then she would tell him of the daily happenings of the farm, of Richard's play and the new words that he had learned to speak, of John's faithful work in the fields and barn, of the everyday things that were the bond between them and that she knew sustained him. And always finding words somehow to cheer him with the love she felt for him and not admit her fears or emptiness. Or write of the hours of wakefulness in the empty bed. Sometimes she would find a labourer from the village who, for a penny, would undertake to pass the letter on to the garrison at Sherborne, and once John took the horse, travelling beyond Yeovil, where he ordered a new blade for the scythe, to take her letter to Francis and bring back word of him.

So the slow heat of August passed into September. Swallows gathered, poised for flight. The days were shortening now, and chill was felt in the twilight air after the sun had dipped beyond the line of trees in the western fields. She knew little of the shift in the momentum of war that was happening to the east of their home. Word of it drifted in from a passing neighbour, a casual labourer who requested a drink and begged for a night's sleep in the barn. Equivocal, unclear, unimaginable to her. For her husband, it was suddenly a reality of action, movement, when the clumsy motions of war they had practised together became the manoeuvres of combat. A large Parliamentary army had been gathered to besiege the town of Sherborne. Appearing cautiously on 2nd September, they were unnerved by the actions of one of the most effective of the Royalist commanders, Sir Ralph Hopton, who led his men to harry the Roundheads whilst the castle was being garrisoned and prepared for siege by the Royalist forces. On the following morning, the Parliamentary army opened fire on the town, but their attack was ill-planned and Hopton had so strategically placed his men that his small force drove them off. They withdrew to their camp, to count their losses. For Francis, it had been his first sour taste of the reality of conflict. The heedless impulse of courage that carried them forward in attack and then the aftermath of success: the pathetic crumpled bodies, both of the dead and the crying, hapless wounded. Hopton determined to press the Parliamentary force further and attacked for several nights under the cover of darkness, causing confusion and terror in the already teetering army of Parliament.

The crisis came soon. Again at night, the Royalist guns fired with such effect of noise and threat, that the destruction and injury caused panic. Hundreds of men deserted and fled from the Parliamentary ranks, and the others who remained presented so demoralised a presence to their officers that they could not be moulded into a fighting force. On 6th September, they dismantled their camp and marched away towards Yeovil, harried as they left by Hopton's troopers.

***

Sometimes, if the wind shifted its direction to come from the east, the thunder of the guns had sounded faintly from the besieged town and Julia and Richard had heard it, perplexed and anxious, on the farm. Then there had been silence for several days, and no news reached them, and her answers to his simple questions were vague and uncertain. The morning of 8th September had begun reluctantly, with the threat of rain that persisted all day. As the hours passed, it had become grey and overcast. A sullen afternoon was moving indistinguishably towards twilight, when there was a sudden split in the cloud, a yellow gash and then a flaring red sun that rolled swiftly down to the horizon. The darkness held back, breathed, and fell on them. As dusk gathered, Nell was outside, as always at this time, standing in the strand of candlelight that stretched from the open door, feeding scraps to the chickens that gathered to the half-chant, half-song of her call. They were pushing one another impatiently, their scaly legs scrabbling, wings ineffectually flapping, beaks dabbing: 'Puck, puck, puck, come on up, come on up, come along, Hedgehop, Greedygut, Feathersoft, Smarteye, Flightyone.' A song of nonsense, a song of contentment, matched by the throaty murmurs of the chickens as they nibbled up the crusts and rinds that she scattered.

There was a movement behind the small barn. Three shadows that rushed at her, scattering the gabbling chickens, grabbing her by the arms, forcing her head back, stifling the screams that brought her father running to her. And he was knocked viciously to the ground, unconscious and her mother came running from the house, calling for her, calling for him. She, too, knocked against the wall of the barn, her head striking the rough stones so that the blood broke out of the gash on her forehead and smeared down the wall as she fell, clutching at its harsh roughness so that her fingers were grazed even as the darkness overtook her. The tallest of the shadows seized the girl, forcing back her flailing, helpless arms and pinioning them behind her as he dragged her into the gloom of the barn and flung her to the earthen floor, kneeling then to pin her down and smother the screams. The other two crowded towards her, breathless with excitement, guilt, horror, they knew not what their emotions were, only the urgency and dominance and throbbing lust of the moment.

'Yours, Will! Time you were a man.' Even as he held down the threshing body of the girl, the leader of them mocked the youngest and the other stood nearby and laughed, high-pitched, as Will struggled to untie his breeches, groping her, hoping for arousal in defiance of his own fear and ignorance and shame. Then, suddenly, he felt under his hands a shift of time and life, realising that she was suffocated, flaccid and fled from them even as he attempted penetration. As Will gasped with a sense of trembling horror, and looked at her face, Amos took his hand from her mouth and her head lolled to the side, her mouth still open in the final empty soundless scream of pain and despair as they had taken from her all seemliness and hope and left her tumbled akimbo in their excited, guilty haste.

The mother stirred, calling, crying, but the young men spurned her roughly aside.

'Leave the old bitch, there's better meat inside,' spat one of them and they ran into and through the house, ransacking, breaking, overturning, smashing, rushing wildly to seek what they could find: valuables to steal, food to seize and cram into desperate mouths, wine and ale to quench a thirst that was unslakeable in its demands. Then they saw the crucifix on the wall above the bed and responded, chanting, as they had learned to do on London streets, 'Papist whore, Jezebel, Papist whore.'

***

Julia has fled with her child to the only secret safety that she knows that is left to her now. Fled from the sound of their staggering footsteps, the smashing and breaking above her head and the loud, harsh voices, to take refuge in the cellar. But they see its dark entrance in the corner of the kitchen and stumble, swearing and clumsy with drink gulped on empty bellies, down the steps. A candle, flaring, held high in the hand of one of them, throws grotesque shadows on the wall. The sound of her heart is like the thunder of those distant guns in her ears and pounds in her throat.

'Hush, hush,' she says, croons, begs, to the child clasped to her, hiding its face in her breast. 'Hush, Richard, Mama's here, Dada will come and save us.'

So they find her, half drunk, half desperate with lust and shame and false zeal that gives them this terrifying immunity. She faces them, cornered, throbbing with terror for him, for herself, and yet filled with courage in her protection of the child.

The three of them now are taking slow, slow, deliberate steps towards her and chanting, 'Royalist whore, Papist bitch, Jezebel, Daughter of Babylon,' again and again as an incantation as they advance. Such a little space across the flags of the cellar, and yet it takes so long to cross them. Trapped against the far wall, she defies them, protecting her two year old son, but they are beside themselves now with dishonour and desire and fervour, and mouthing insults and slogans gather round her to take her. To seize and cast aside the child and then attack and rape the mother. But she refuses to let go, and as they attempt to break the child from her she bites one of the men's hands (young men, she realises even at that moment, scarcely old enough to bear arms) and he in a confused rage, knocks her against the wall and then stabs the child, and through the child, her body. They thrust her aside, to collapse against the wall, the child under her as she drops cracking his head on the stones as they fall together, love-locked in dying. They take her rings, breaking her fingers in their panicked haste, then thrust through the cellar door back into the room above, pausing only to seize money from the chest upstairs before they run away, feet stumbling over the paved yard.

Soon, only the swift darkness and the quiet remain, to melt back over the desecration that they have left behind them.

Suddenly they feel the coldness of the evening air and the heat and passion ebbs from them, leaving them sickened and chilled, running and running from the house and the shadowed barn. Running, panting for breath until the grey light of morning hunts for them and drives them into a thin clump of woodland where they seek to hide, gasping, swearing, their fingers clutching the rough bark of trees, their faces pressed against the crook of their arms as they struggle for breath, struggle to find the words to cover the shared degradation. Vagrants and outlaws now, deserters from an army they believed to have been scattered and amongst folk here in the West known to be loyal to the king. They must move stealthily, hiding in the countryside by day and moving east until they can forget their shame, if they ever can, and rejoin the army of Parliament in some new campaign, far away.

***

Stirring in the darkened yard as the sound of the running feet and the hoarsely gasping haste fades, the parents find the body of the broken, suffocated maid, and then, searching within the house, their mistress and the child. They hold each other's hands in speechless sorrow. Stooping, wordless, they carry the body of their daughter into the farmhouse and cover it. In the first light of morning, and then only very slowly, are they able to walk together through the darkness of the lanes, to go to Sherborne to seek their master, begging for entry at the castle gateway, sent from soldier to soldier until he is found. Francis, requesting leave from his commanding officer, and finding somewhere a horse to hire for them to ride back together, returned with them to the house, aware that their hesitant words and silences were hiding a horror worse than he could imagine. He found his wife and son where they had been flung in the corner of the cellar, stiffened with death, encircled together. He lifted them, stiff in his arms, embracing them now, so light, so remote from him.

He placed her and their child gently on the ledge in the far corner of the cellar. 'Build up the wall,' he said to John, and he did not know then or afterwards what kind of madness made him say it. 'Build it and hide her safely here.' Her still cold body, rigidly enclosing the child, was unresponsive to his lips, his hands. The front of her bodice was stained with the effusion of her blood. 'The liquefaction of her clothes,' he said, softly at first. Then again, 'The liquefaction of her clothes,' with a kind of terrible silent laughter shaking his diaphragm as the horror took hold of him. Strange images walked in his mind: the raising of Lazarus, and the emergence into the light of the once-dead and himself greeting them, seeing them restored. Whether he would tear down the wall with eager hands and find them wonderfully alive, or after his own death, return to them and summon them forth to join him, he did not know. His mind had fallen into chaos. So, defying reasoned thought and the conventions of piety, he laid them hastily yet gently on the ledge that was raised above the floor, the mother encircling the child she had sought to protect. Within a little leather bag he placed his rings and the miniature of himself, breaking the locket apart as he took it from her neck, her father's gift, hiding it in the breast of her dress, next to her heart, next to that terrible wound. The picture of herself he took gently from her, the links of the gold chain still bloodied, hanging it around his neck. 'I will return to you,' he murmured, kissing her brow, her lips, the child's cold cheeks. 'All my treasure is here.'

'Build up the wall. Let her lie here, with him. Let no-one touch her.' The passion of his own grief had blinded him to the agony of his servants, but now he saw them afresh. John, holding the hand of his wife. Trembling. Old suddenly, as if the strength of their years had been sucked from them.

'But Master, shouldn't I fetch parson?' John spoke hesitantly.

'No! She needs no prayers to send her safe to God,' he said bitterly. 'I will not have that man near her. Ezekiel Cropper with his lies and strictures and hatred of all things free and beautiful. If I return, that will be time enough to make her a memorial.' He paused. 'Pray for her soul and for the boy,' he said, softening, as he saw the devotion as well as the horror in the older man's eyes. 'She would have thanked you for your care. As I do. Pray for them, as I will pray for the soul of your dear Nell, sent innocent on her way to God. Bury your dear, dead daughter. Care for the beasts. Live here.' His voice was tight, forced through the impossible stricture of his throat. 'I am returning to the war, and I pray to God I find the ones who did this thing.'

He helped them to carry the tender body of their daughter onto the table where she could be washed and shrouded and mourned. Then he rode off, turning in his saddle to see them in the doorway, huddled and diminished by sorrow. He must tell the old man, her father. He barely knew how that could be done. And as he rode, the rhythm of the horse's hooves was like the pulse of his own heart, Harvey's pulse, he remembered, that sent the blood on its constant and essential journey. He realised he could not speak her name aloud, nor the child's, although they ran in his head like water..."In silks my Julia goes... the liquefaction of her clothes." But now the blood had stiffened that had run, had gushed down, mingling

Richard and Julia, Richard and Julia. "The liquefaction of her clothes..." The half-crazed iteration accompanied the beat of his horse's hooves.

He only knew that after he had told her father, he must rejoin the king's army of the West Country and seek to be thereafter posted to Sir Ralph Hopton's Regiment if it were possible. There stood the most chance of action. Changed in an instant, he would become a silent, preoccupied trooper, quick to volunteer, suddenly hardened both to the brutalities of war and in the endurance of privation as the campaign moved further west into winter.

Chapter Eight

Francis, Sidney

Francis left his horse in the yard of the *George Inn*, walking the few, familiar, now inexorable steps down the street to the beloved house. He found the old man, his father-in-law, sitting as he so often sat, half-turned to the window to look out over the garden, his flexible hands resting on the dark wood of the arms of the great chair, the carved tendrils of vine smoothed to gold by the habitual caress of his fingers. At the sound of Francis' voice he began to rise to his feet, turning from the dull light of the day, delighted to greet a man who was closer to him than his own absent sons.

'Francis! My dear son! I knew you were with the garrison of the town, and the rebels have fled, but I did not dream of seeing you so soon.' He smiled with the pleasure of the greeting, but something in the bleak, fixed pallor of Francis' face touched him with foreboding and he fumbled for the arms of his chair and sat down, suddenly strengthless and afraid.

There were few words needed between them, beyond the severe truth of what had happened. The horror of what he had seen was in Francis' eyes and the trembling of his mouth. The old man read his face, held his shaking hands, then groped his way out of the chair and towards the window as though he might still see his child come running, laughing, back to him across the grass. They stood together, their silent grief clawing at their hearts, shared, but unendurable.

Francis left at last to return to his commanding officer. Whatever dreary light had coloured the day was draining away now and rain was threatening in clouds that massed against the skyline. The maidservant opened the door but he brushed by her, wordlessly, and strode down the path. The whole household knew that some great trouble had visited them and they were almost afraid, the maid and the manservant, to enter the chamber where their master sat, and offer lights and wine and food. And when they did so, after many minutes had passed, they could not at first discern what had happened. He sat silent, a motionless dull silhouette against grey windows, his head leaning against the chair back, as Francis had left him, but now one hand lolled from the armrest. Then they came near, and the candle the maid held aloft showed him to them. His face was pewter coloured, and dreadfully sagging, as though the weight of what the heart and brain carried had brought about a landslide of grief, carrying half his face, his shoulder, arm and leg down with it. The left eye was closed, the mouth skewed and slumped, the left hand fallen nervelessly from the chair. One eye stared fixedly at them, beyond recognition. Bending over him, with dread and tenderness, they could barely hear the sounds he could still make. His words were slurred without the framing rationality of consonants, as the lips failed him. Only vowels: 'oo, ee, ah.' Repeated and repeated, moaning, gentle, hopeless.

It took time for news to reach them from the village and when it came it was so sparse and confused that they could barely understand what had happened. It came as rumour to the marketplace and spread from mouth to mouth with the eagerness of horror: the old couple Marjory and John grieving their dead daughter; their mistress and the small child vanished and the master gone away to war to find the renegades who had done this thing. By the time they had understood what little truth could be gleaned amidst the details of embellished dread and invective, their own master was fading fast. Locked in his bed by the paralysis that had fallen on him, he lay unresponsive, barely drinking from the cup they held to his mouth, and refusing all food. In what was left of his mind and strength, he sought the mercy of death, and found it mildly waiting for him within a week. They sent word to the sons in London, but across counties now subject to war and turmoil, the message was lost. And so, Julian Richard Glover was buried without his sons' dissembled grief and without their wrangling over the terms of his will.

***

John and Marjory had carried the body of their daughter on a flimsy hurdle to the village a mile or so away. They stumbled with weary grief at each step, and were unable to speak to share the burden of sorrow or the aftermath of the terror and pain that they had both suffered. Neighbours gathered them in, reading the heart without words and knowing the childless years and the longing and delight of their child, who now lay huddled and still before them. Parson Cropper, compassionate, despite the rigour of his teachings, buried her safe in the churchyard, and sought to give the comfort of resignation to both husband and wife. But they stared at him, dumb and remote.

Four days had passed since they had been struck down,

bruised, terrified, grief-stricken, with wounds to the heart and memory that could have no healing. John, seeking to comfort his wife, through gesture, through the tenderness with which he tried to persuade her to eat and drink, found that he had lost all words, all thought beyond their immediate survival. For many days he shared that place of his master's tormented madness, a place where time was suspended, where decay and loss might be denied and the dead wait for a re-awakening like the story of Lazarus. So it was not difficult for him to tell no-one of the demand that Francis had made, nor of the fate of his mistress and the child. John returned to the farmhouse to build the wall as he had been told, taking the brick and stone from the tumbled derelict outhouses that had waited to be restored. Working swiftly, he walled in those interwoven bodies with a single thickness of rough laid stone and bricks and clumsy lime mortar. As he worked, he could not look at them, afraid perhaps that what he did was against all Christian teaching, afraid that the pity of it would overwhelm him, together with the grievous death of his own Nell. To him they were all one. Caught up and drowned in a torrent of hate and cruelty that he could not understand. He spoke prayers for them, leaning against the pillar to the right of the completed but still unstable wall, prayers half remembered from the recent burial service, half remembered from a lifetime of church going. His mind fixed and held on one phrase, one repeated phrase that held him then and enabled him to bear his own heart's grief and carry his wife through all the days that lay ahead: "Have mercy".

'Have mercy. Have mercy on us,' he said again and again as he thought of those three tender lives, and of the stern young husband, suddenly aged and unwavering, who had ridden off to seek revenge.

Neither he nor Marjory could bear to live at the farmhouse.

Its yard, doors, rooms, were stained with memory. They stayed in the village, taken in by Marjory's family until they could find a small place of their own. For some months John returned to the farm daily, seeing the locked farmhouse turn blind with neglect and filled only with the slow, sifting dust. As winter encroached, the barely planted garden and orchard lost definition under sprawling weeds and brown, sodden, fallen leaves. Behind the wall, the bodies began to shrink into what would become a skeletal casket in the sealed dry air and the leather bag, holding its treasure of the broken locket and rings would slowly fall into the space vacated by the once beating heart. Their clothing steadily disintegrated and faded into sparse threads; all its gloss and texture would diminish unseen as the months, and later the years, turned.

John tended the animals as autumn laid its chill hand upon the farm, bringing them within the barn as the weather turned wet and sullen and turning the hay so that what they fed on was full of late sweetness and spreading the straw so that it was warm and clean. The innocent gabble of the chickens mocked him with echoes of his daughter's calls and he took them to the village to sell, trusting that his master would understand. Yet he could not manage the winter ploughing alone and knew that the fields would lie barren. As time moved on, he fell into a simple pattern of duty: he checked the beasts, the fences and ditch sides and worked with his neighbours and wherever else he could, to pick up a day's casual labour to dig or mend. He kept food enough, but only enough, on their table, but neither he nor Marjory seemed to care any longer.

***

Francis strode away from his father-in-law's house to

collect his horse and return to the Royalist camp at Sherborne Castle, riding out east from the town. He left familiar boyhood and lovers' streets behind and entering the great southwest gate of the castle to rejoin his company. But no longer now as an unsure, untried horseman. No longer the young man who, only weeks before, had come to the garrison at Sherborne. Then he had come as a trooper, seeking no rank, bringing no tenantry with him. A simple loyalty. Obedience to a distant king, glimpsed across a crowd in his Whitehall Palace all those years ago. Probably too, he had realised then, an affectionate memory of Sidney who would also be responding with devotion to this cause. A cause that had felt in the early days to be illusory, remote, its ideologies and compulsions, its city tumult, very far from this green landscape of ancient herding and harvesting.

In those hot, still days of August and September the war had seemed unreal to him, less real than the daily heat and flies, the hours of training, the unaccustomed rub of leather and steel. There had been a slow gathering of men to Sherborne and the castle was garrisoned for siege if need be, with defensive positions set up in the town. There they had waited in the summer sunshine, with the scents of harvest drifting to them, the rhythmic swing of the long scythes glimpsed on the hillsides. There was a harvest to gather; grain and fodder to store. Beasts to tend. Here in the west surely men would drift away from the colours and shake their heads as if over a strange and passing dream and return to their farms and fields and barns. Francis found it hard to believe that such remote causes: taxation, religious practices, the supremacy of king or Parliament, should bring fellow countrymen to war. Yet he had seen in the London streets the potential for violence, the ravening hunger for dominance. He had seen crowds swayed by oratory, moving as one creature to turn and devour their opponents. He had heard the language of fanaticism: it should not have surprised him that it would spill into open conflict.

Newly recruited, he had known enough in those early days to be able to perform the simple manoeuvres of cavalry movement that he had learned in the trained bands as a youth and in Oxford. To guide the horse with his knees, the hands free to reach for the flintlock pistol or the heavy sword with the rounded guard over the hand. The sword that he had felt to be clumsy and lifeless, reluctant, only days and hours before. Now it was as if it had been re-forged; now it was an extension of his arm, its weight potent, mortal.

His mind was closed to conscious, voluntary thought, yet invaded by constant, interwoven impressions: vivid threads of memory, images of their blood and the touch of their cold unresponsive limbs and hands and faces. It was as if a shard of pain was now lodged beneath his breastbone. A grim, fixed determining of revenge. He returned his mount to the picket lines and saw that it was well rubbed down and fed, leaning his head against his horse's ribs to draw its strength into himself, to feel the fusion of its sweat and the shudder of its breath and heartbeat as his own. Any, all, activity was grateful to him now, tiring the body so that the mind might rest. He reported for duty, avoiding the kind enquiries, the offer of relief. When he saw his commanding officer he asked for action, for a swift transfer to whichever company would be the first to engage the enemy. Wherever there could be hard-riding, demanding, consuming involvement. Action that would give him no respite, no space for thoughts or grief that might sap and diminish him. Sir Ralph Hopton, already identified as a commander of flair and action, took him into his company, and he rode with him immediately to Yeovil, first to reconnoitre and then to his first real blooding, a taste of conflict that came near defeat, though the Roundheads left Yeovil and marched away to Dorchester. Then followed a fruitless weary march to Minehead, before the Royalist army divided, with Hopton directed to take the Horse through north Devon to cross the Tamar near its source and so come into Cornwall, believed to be loyal to the king.

Turning from the coast and the wide red sands of Minehead, they must now skirt the forbidding heights of Exmoor as the weather turned to deeper autumn. This was a landscape unfamiliar to Francis, of louring forests, bare moor and rough, coarse grassland and sedge, and rushing waters that stormed down steep crevasses of rock. Herds of wild ponies were sighted in the mist, appearing at first glimpse to be clouded phantoms, yet they were standing stolid against the driving rain. As the weather roughened, the company of Foot and Horse clung tenaciously to the slippery tracks of reddening mud that ran parallel to the coast. Grinding uphill at Porlock, and then down: repeated patterns of fatigue. Hill climbs and descents, men and horses, pack animals and baggage wagons, through Lynton, and, with glimpses on scouting expeditions of the jagged black rocks of the bays of north Devon, on to Barnstaple.

Rain swept sideways from the Bristol Channel, penetrating the chinks of garments and glove, chafing the line of leather on the thigh, and making wretched the exhausted cavalry horses and the ponies of the baggage train. Welcomed and rejected in turn, seizing food and fodder if it were not offered, with promises of distant future repayment. A trail of trampled, rutted lanes, slithering in mud, marked their passage. Farmers gathered in their sheep to hide them away from them, and to right and left, the sodden traces of the harvest reminded many of fields untended, of beasts abandoned. Then onwards: to cross the threading line of the infant Tamar River, trampling over moorland of rush and gully until at last rising up to crest the hills above Youlstone and then to the village of Kilkhampton, and to encamp in the Royalist estate of Sir Bevil Grenville. Francis had lost count of the days of hard riding. Around one hundred and thirty miles. No intent but endurance with daily fortitude and then to find the ease that comes with exhaustion. There had been as yet no further encounters with the enemy, whom Francis could now see only as faceless, clumped, featureless. And believed capable of all cruelties.

So ensued, through all the wet daylight hours of October, the move and counter move of troops through waterlogged lanes, and the daily management of weary men and horses. Francis learned the imperative of supplies and rest to an army on the move. For the trooper, obedience to a greater strategy required no thought, just the constant endurance of slumped fatigue, the long rides of saddle-sore discomfort, of leather sodden and rubbing at the groin and inner thigh, just as the weight of a buff coat worried at the skin of throat and shoulder. Each day the discipline of keeping weapons bright and serviceable, learning to bind the horses' harnesses with rags to stop the chink, chink of riding through darkened lanes. Over miles, over days, each day alike in its doggedness, relieved only by a sudden skirmish of energy and hate and violence and in its aftermath he would subside into the empty weariness of survival.

In those days of hand to hand, rushed and bitter fighting, he learned more urgently than any anatomist the archways of life, where the sticky exuberance would flow from severed vessels. Those exits of the gush of bright arterial blood that Harvey had described so carefully. The cusp of the throat, the point above the steel and leather jerkin; the armpit, as the arm was raised to thrust. He learned to guard against the jab to the groin or the thigh. And to guard himself also from seeing faces; to see only the separate components, eyes, brows, mouth, so that none connected to form any identity that might become a man like himself: husband, lover, father, son.

Then, at last, after many days, it came to him with a sense of fitness, a right order in things that Francis should meet with Sidney Godolphin after a day's hard riding. Settling and tending his own horse in the picket lines, he heard a familiar voice among the newly joined company that had come from further west. Sidney had come up from his own town of Helston, bringing his tenantry with him. Men who were loyal to him, willing to serve as he served among them, without claiming rank, but riding as a trooper. So there was a renewal of their friendship, bringing, as it had done on each occasion, an awareness of a destined pattern of meetings. Whenever they could, they chose to ride side by side, often in silence. Only after many days could Francis speak of what had happened at the farm, of his wife and son, of his quest for revenge. Yet, though he did not realise it, the release of words began to soften the rigid hatreds that had made him reckless and implacable, a stern, isolated young man, whom his fellow soldiers had learned to leave to himself at times when they themselves had been glad of the companionship of a shared, snatched meal or drink, a communal jest or story.

Sidney said little. He listened, accepted. Just once, he spoke, comprehending all, yet without judgement: 'Hatred is a cold bed-fellow,' he said to Francis.

Sidney, Francis thought. *He does not, as others do, walk within the shadows of his own mortality. He is too free and life-*

loving for that. His grave compassion is real and genuinely felt, yet his presence cheers and revives wherever he goes.

Gradually, as the days passed, Francis released himself to this trusted friendship, even to the renewal of feeling that it brought. Around him, others noticed his hesitant and gradual inclusion in the exchange of news about the slow campaign in the west, and in the necessary comradeship of tired men seeking ease and safety.

Slowly, the year drew to its close in darkening nights and sharp cold. A season of campaigning, indecisive, bloody and wasteful. Both armies had struggled for the control of the River Tamar and the roads to Plymouth and its vital source of supplies from the sea, but neither had mastery. The Royalist army foundered on the brink of dismemberment. Men, far from home, short of winter clothing and equipment, often unpaid, struggled to believe in a cause, a remote purpose, when all was so uncertain. Only the loyalties of men to individual leaders whom they knew and followed, as Sidney's tenants' loyalties remained steadfast to him, enabled the army to hold together as the days shortened.

Francis had learned a new landscape, strange to him, of towering rocks and heights, clefts and rushing waters, forest and heath. In these months of winter, the once purple heather had browned to sodden entwined treachery to hoof and foot. He remembered the red soil and rocks as they had entered Devon: now the soil gave way to rock and rush and bog, and half wild sheep that scrambled away from them with staring eyes. The landscape had changed from the open salver of land of his own familiar Levels and the clear heights that lay to the east that had been shaped by ancient men; changed from the wooded slopes of beech and lanes of high hawthorn hedges and banks. Here, small fields had been scraped from heather and bracken and sown in hopes of a meagre harvest. But that autumn there had been the tramping of men and horse across the Tamar, taking rest and reinforcements in Cornwall and then pushing back into Devon to attack the enemy. Such costly movement of men had wasted scant harvests, leaving fields un-scythed, or churned to a morass by horse and man in the advance and sway of battle. And in the wake of the fighting, the reddened, battered, trampled straw.

A strange, instinctive, unspoken truce brought a lull in the fighting towards the end of December. That Christmas, they encamped near Bodmin, the men and their horses in barns; their officers in local inns or billeted in homes, or welcomed at the house of squire or parson. It was a season of such cold that it seemed to root itself in their bodies. There was a temporary respite from the movement and uncertainty of battle, a time when men might draw together in war's unique and intimate comradeship. Around the evening fires, the flickering light delineated features in amber, red and black, capturing the glint of an eye, a buckle, a sword hilt, the ring on a finger. They were men who dwelt together only in the whereabouts of today, not knowing how long this conflict might continue, or to what end. It was unthinkable that the king's majesty should lose, and be made subject to whatever terms were set by those who opposed him. Yet it had been inconceivable only months ago that a king should be at war with his people, and be so vehemently opposed. There was a sense of unreality about the present scene, a sense that this was only a prelude to an unimaginable play. Francis saw again, in the eye of memory, the pale oval of the king's face: the eyebrows arched in perpetual astonishment, the trim beard, the delicacy of lace and gleam of satin.

We fight for a dream, he thought, with troubled

presentiment, *a phantom. It holds sway over us because we cannot imagine the upheaval of a new order of government or the chaos and lawlessness that will follow. What was it that Sidney had quoted, so long ago, in the parry and thrust of argument over Hobbes' principles of government? '"Take but degree away, untune that string, and, hark, what discord follows!"'* Now, he realised, they were living in that state of mutiny, where "appetite, a universal wolf" had made all things his "universal prey".

He could not shake from him the thoughts that suddenly crowded in. That wolf-like savagery had come too near to him and now he allowed his mind to linger on the tragedy that had driven him to endure every day until this day with terrible and ruthless energy. The cruelty and excess of the young men had been described to him in the hoarse fragmented words of his servant, John. Men, perhaps much younger than himself, scarcely more than boys, yet pitiless, violating home and all sanctity, slaughtering innocence. He had sought for them in the ranks of the Parliamentary army, believing that some instinct would show him who they were, so that he might be avenged. But now he knew that search to be in vain. They would not have lingered in the West Country, deserters who might be recognised and punished. They would have fled east, back to their old haunts, perhaps to enlist again, unknown, under a new commander. Men from the east, London maybe, John had told him, young men of sharp, harsh voices: strangers.

He knew also that cruelty and excess was not limited to the Parliamentary army; men of his own side were capable of rape and theft and all brutality. Some officers winked at it, calling it the spoils of war, but others punished such crimes severely with flogging, and hanging was not unknown. They were reminded often that the West Country was loyal to the king and its people must be treated with gentleness, even though an army moving through the villages and small towns must inevitably take and devour livestock, fodder, food and ale. It must demand provisions and shelter for men and horses for its survival. The countryside lay stripped behind them, the harvest robbed, the people impoverished, close to famine if the spring did not bring them hope. He remembered certain dreadful words from the Book of Revelation quoted with fervour by street preachers. Now The Rider of the Pale Horse had been let loose, to kill with sword and famine and pestilence, and by the wild beasts. He saw his own small farm, violated as it had been and now empty of its small numbers of cattle and sheep and the fields naked and unploughed, returning to waste and barrenness. If the king's army had not already taken all, then the army of Parliament had overrun much of Somerset and it would have fallen prey to them. There would be no sowing now. He prayed, if his prayers might still be heard, that John and his wife were safe and able somehow to exist on what little was left to them, and were not utterly broken by the loss of their beloved daughter. Their loss, like his, was unspeakable.

There are times of companionship known only to fighting men, who inhabit solely the one present instant of sensation and consider neither past nor future. The comfortable warmth of food and drink in the belly after hardship. The ease of shoulder and arm at rest, thighs and legs released from the rigour of the saddle and the day's forced ride or the weary march through bleak countryside. Slight wounds, now easing from smart. The rub of a friend's shoulder against your own. The fire catches, the heat springs up and flames colour pale and weary faces with an illusion of health. Tonight, thank God, it does not rain, though the frost is sharp and the leaves cluttered on the grass are crisping with the bitterness of cold, and each is edged with fine white crystals. Stars are breaking through the dark: familiar clusters of constellations, patterns of timeless guidance, silver and unattainable. Francis sat alongside Sidney that night, that Christmas Eve, and there was some singing, then silence. Men were thinking of home, of families, of loss, of the hope of peace. Of the Christ child born among men. Or had He sickened of their endless brutal violence and left them, Francis wondered? Not far away, in the camp of the enemy, they too would remember the birth and share these thoughts and hopes. Maybe they too would sing, if it was not forbidden to them to sing the old songs of Mary and her child.

Later that evening, Christ's Mass evening, they refreshed the fires, waiting for the service that would lead them to the local church at midnight and the great mystery of the Eucharist. As they waited, someone began a song, and then another. Ancient songs learned who knows when, known from childhood, bringing a comfort out of the past: 'As Joseph was a-walking, he heard an angel sing.' Sometimes they joined in, sometimes a solo voice. Sidney sang, out of long ago, 'I sing of a maiden who is matchless, King of all Kings to her son she chose.'

Later, when silence fell, Francis stirred, needing to recall some sense of faith, some hope. 'Sidney,' he whispered, 'tell us something, remind us, read us a verse of your own.'

And Sidney looked around the group, seeing into their silence and doubt and spoke from memory.

'Lord when the wise men came from far
Led to thy Cradle by a Star,
Then did the shepherds too rejoice,
Instructed by thy Angel's voice,
Blest were the wise men in their skill,
And shepherds in their harmless will.

Wise men in tracing nature's laws
Ascend unto the highest cause,
Shepherds with humble fearfulness
Walk safely, though their light be less:
Though wise men better know the way
It seems no honest heart can stray.'

In the days that followed, Francis held those words as a faint light in his own inner darkness, stumbling as he was with the weariness of hatred, the purposelessness of continuing to seek revenge. "Shepherds with humble fearfulness walk safely, though their light be less ... it seems no honest heart can stray". He had knelt that night for Communion on the hard flagstones of the church, the cold driving through the stuff of his breeches until it seemed that it would freeze and lock bone and joint. And the words of the General Confession moved him with a new consciousness of the huge burden of his vengeance, and its futility, and how far it had taken him from the tenderness of love that he had felt for wife and child and made him a stranger to himself. The familiar words of penitence came to him, giving utterance at last to the burden of the heart. "Have mercy on us, have mercy on us", ran through his head like water.

Sleepless, Francis thought of the home he knew he would not see again. Whatever happened to him, it would never be a place of welcome. His own grief had consumed him, making him blind to others. Now he saw and felt with utter clarity the anguish of his servants, John and his wife Marjory, and the agony to them of the loss of their daughter, Nell, scarcely more than a child. She had come to them late in life after years of diminishing hope, and now had been stolen from them and in such a manner. He saw, too, his own madness in the concealment of his wife and child. What did he hope for? That in some miraculous way he would return, break down the wall and clasp in his arms a living wife, a living child? Unchanged? A Winter's Tale of resurrection? His mind brought back to him his last glimpse of them, locked together in love and death. And with them, the image of his mother as he imagined her, enfolding the stillborn baby as he longed to believe she had been buried.

In the heavy darkness long before any glimpse of the break of day he was roused to join the sentries that kept ceaseless watch. He went alone to tend his horse and saddle up. Before mounting, he leaned his head against its flank. Pressed against the coarse hair to stifle the sound, he found that he could weep, for John and Marjory and for Nell, for his wife, Julia and for his son, Richard, naming them at last. And for himself. Then for all that was lost already in this war and all that would be lost, before it was over.

***

The year turned: a New Year, 1643, bringing with it news that rippled through the ranks: the queen's majesty was seeking aid in the Netherlands and might any day bring fresh resources to the Royalist cause. But Sir Thomas Fairfax had moved with decisive success in the West Riding to advance the Parliamentary cause in the north. Wars and rumours of wars. In the west the campaigning season must be further extended into winter. As the ground froze, so movement eased and Sir Ralph Hopton, now recognised as the outstanding leader of the western Royalist army, gathered his forces. The Parliamentary army also ably led and well-resourced was growing in strength and vying for dominance of the West Country: Cornwall, loyal to the king, must form not only an enclave of resistance, but the ground from which a strengthened army might grow to retake the West and hold it secure.

Hopton's raids across the Tamar to the north of Plymouth had proved a provocation to the Parliamentary cause, forcing them to send significant troops and forces by sea so effectively that an attempt to blockade and hold Plymouth failed. Attempts at the end of December to take Exeter had been thwarted, and a demoralised Royalist army was forced to retreat to Cornwall. As January began, diminishing supplies, the hardship of the weather, the dejection of the men, put all at risk, but hopes were revived by Cornish loyalty in the face of attack, firstly at Bridestow and then countering the abortive Parliamentary attack on Saltash.

The marching men and cavalry were only aware of the endurance of each dull hour. The greater strategy lay in their commanders' hands. For the fighting men, there were constant indistinguishable days of movement regardless of the weather; advance against an outpost of the enemy and then fall back. Losses and wounds; uncertainty; cold; hunger. Hopton drew his troops back to Bodmin and regrouped, and the Cornishmen gathered to him. But at Liskeard, less than thirty miles away to the east, the Parliamentary commander, General Ruthin, waited in the expectation of a decisive and victorious campaign.

Suddenly all was changed. On 17th January, a ferocious storm drove three Parliamentary warships into the Royalist port of Falmouth, where they were immediately seized with their lading of equipment and treasure, which rapidly rearmed and revitalised the Cornish army. Hopton, confirmed as Commander-in-Chief, determined on a direct attack on the enemy, leading his army out to new quarters at Boconnoc, northeast of Lostwithiel. The next day, 19th January, the armies met at Braddock Down, drawn up on opposite sides of the valley. For two hours Francis watched, holding his mount in check as minor volleys between the musketeers of both sides made little difference, but then Hopton unmasked his concealed, though limited, artillery and sent shots to tear with fear and wounding into the enemy ranks, before unleashing both cavalry and infantry. The Roundheads turned after firing a scattered volley and fled, to be relentlessly pursued through narrow lanes, with fiercely fought clashes of cavalry charges and hand to hand fighting with pike, short sword and musket between those on foot. A grim encounter, with wounded and dead on both sides. At length Francis and his troop turned back, exhausted, bloodied, leaving others to the pursuit. The Parliamentary force fled all the way to Liskeard, where the townsfolk rose against them and many were captured, together with arms and equipment. A retreating and terrorised army. The tide of war in the west had turned.

Hopton led his army to storm Saltash, four days later, with extraordinary success, and with the aim of marching to encircle Plymouth. Here he was held in check; his Cornish soldiers, most of whom had never travelled before beyond their villages, were reluctant to cross into Devon, across the boundary of the Tamar. To attack Plymouth would over extend his resources, but Hopton decided to encircle and blockade the vital port. The war then became for Francis and Sidney, among the cavalry, one of reactive movement: effective, fluid attacks wherever Parliamentary attempts were made to take and hold the roads or bridges that led to the port. Strategic places like Okehampton, the river crossing at Chagford, the bridge at Kingsbridge, must be held. To the north lay the unassailable high moors and forest of Dartmoor. An unyielding mass of rocks and crags, steep clefts and gullies, treacherous to man and horse. No tracks known, except to those whose ancestors had herded animals on its barrenness and passed their ancient secrets on. Neither army could hope to cross, but must skirt its edge. The vital roads that ran at its border and the bridges and fords that gave access to the south were the key to the west and to its ports, Plymouth and Falmouth, and between them the towns of Liskeard, Lothwithiel, Bodmin, Truro.

***

That February they rode together, Francis and Sidney, under the leadership of Sir John Berkeley, who had built a swift reputation for effective and gallant attack in his successful assault on Kingsbridge. Their orders were to bring reinforcements to Okehampton, so vital to the western roads that circled the high moor, and to attack the Roundheads at Chagford where they had sought to establish a garrison, to control the passage of the River Teign. They halted to camp that February night in abandoned barns and outhouses, under the lee, though they did not know it, of ancient settlements and hut circles high on the stone hills above them.

All day they had ridden east through crooked narrow lanes in sharp Devon valleys, between high banks of rock and trees, with overgrown, clinging fibrous nettles and clawing bramble that whipped and scratched man and horse. Always, the sodden relentless rain and in their ears the rush of water in the valley bottoms. Above them, the grim rise to the moors and the tangling roots of heather, the deceitful glimmer of bright green grass and rush, masking the slipping edge of bog that could, and did, suck horse and rider into its moist viridian and orange lips.

That evening, the seventh day of the month, they settled their horses, and turned to find what warmth and food they could, lighting reluctant fires in the shelter of stone walls and dripping oaks, before they must ride perilously through the dark to attack at dawn. Sidney was singing under his breath a song from the days of the old queen, Queen Elizabeth, "The Silver Swan".

'The silver swan, who living had no note,
When death approached unlocked her silent throat:
Leaning her breast against the reedy shore
Thus sang her first and last and sung no more.
Farewell all joys, come death and close my eyes.
More geese than swans now live, more fools than wise.'

The single line of melody, sung without the interweaving of madrigal voices, carried great solitude of feeling, an aching of regret.

'I do not see an end to it, Francis,' he said quietly, rubbing with a scrap of soft leather the chased silver mountings of the pistols he carried. 'I cannot see an end. A dreaming king who sees a divine authority in his rule that draws him to martyrdom like a lodestone. An obdurate Parliament, and an army of malcontents and preachers, but there is steel among them. Steel and purpose and fearlessness. But fanaticism too and hatred and cruelty and the destruction of beauty and all that is of the past. I do not see where this will end, until this nation is ravaged, and weary with war. And loss and waste.'

Francis struggled to speak the words that clogged his mouth. 'I came to it in hate and for revenge. Duty first, all those months ago. Loyalty to the king's cause. What else would I do? But it seems so long ago now. Summer, a harvest wasted, winter. Hatred and revenge. But even that has gone. I killed so many, and did not see their faces. As if I had been sightless.' He stared into the darkness that waited restlessly beyond the circle of the fire. 'Then, days ago, I saw one, looked and saw him, before he died. Young, frightened, in terrible pain as he fell away from my wounding.'

There was silence between them before Francis' disconnected and halting phrases stumbled towards their conclusion.

'Nor I,' he said, looking steadily now at his companion. 'I do not know how it will end. For me, nor for any of us.' In the uttering of the words, the energy, the purposes of hate, had drained away from him. In his mind now rose, like a pale misshapen moon, the haunting ovoid face of the king, disembodied above the lace edged collar, the dark doublet.

A brief respite, food, and the horses fed and rested, then the fires were smothered, and they set out in the darkness. They rode at a steady trot whenever possible, but more often slowed to walking pace through the constricted defiles of steep and hidden valleys that plunged down from the barren and treacherous moorland above. They rode all through the early hours of the night, following crooked tracks of sliding mud, men and horses pressed together by the encroaching banks of snagging stem and branch. Sharp declines, then the pull upward to the heights above the small town of Chagford and its vital river crossing: key to the web of roads that held the West country in their mesh.

Dawn had greyed the sky as they dropped down through narrow lanes to surprise the small Roundhead garrison recently quartered there. A fast-running brawl between men hastily mounted from their billets in taverns and barns and now driven up the street to the church, high towered above the town. Then spilling violently into the graveyard, encircled by dripping sycamore trees, and into the courtyard of the inn opposite. Scarce room to stab and thrust, still less to load and fire once the first volley of pistol was discharged. The shouts of men and the bawled defiant watchwords of their causes, the screeching neighs of horses, and the screams of men, who fell sometimes to be trampled under the great hooves of their mounts that were maddened by fear and by the scent of blood.

Passing beneath the high church tower, Francis urged his horse forward towards the stand of trees above a narrow lane that fell sharply away to the valley. Sidney, close beside him, had been injured, shot by a chance musket ball from the church tower, yet still clinging precariously to his horse with the momentum that had swept them all on, clattering up the steep street by the church to gain the advantage of the high ground. As they gained the woodland, he fell from his horse to roll helplessly as frantic hooves clashed about his head and shoulders. Francis, too, alongside him, had been relentlessly pursued to the copse until he was overtaken and a sword thrust caught him beneath the skirt of his buff coat, sudden and deep into the femoral artery. He swayed from the saddle to crash among the leaves and branches of the undergrowth as the fighting drove over his head and away up the hillside.

'There's life in him,' they said above his head, a little later, but not of him, and they disentangled and lifted Godolphin's body away from his, taking him into the courtyard of the nearby inn and under the curved arch of its doorway to die slowly, bravely, of unstaunched wounds that leaked into the floor where he lay. Francis heard them, though in what sense he was aware or alive, he did not know. The frozen earth had cleaved to his body, penetrating skin to the bone, stilling pulse and all the gushing bright crimson movement of his life. A hand was pressed against his breastbone to feel the absent rhythm of his heart. 'He's gone then,' someone said, and they lifted him to lie with the others, few and futile, at the edge of the thicket. Hands took from him all that would be of use: the sword still clenched in his right hand; his pistols and gauntlets, his boots and stiff leather jacket. Somewhere in the distance his horse snickered and he knew he would be led away and another would take him into future battle. Fingers, not yet calloused by war, lingered over the locket that fell through the untied linen shirt at his throat, and turned it face down upon his breast and laced the shirt over it, leaving it with him to fall into the earth. Then his comrades left him.

The skirmish became a faltering brawl, and then a clamour of shouts and of horses' hoof beats skidding down the narrow street in pursuit. The retreating Roundhead force fled back through the town and scattered into the woodland to regroup and take to the lanes by night. The Royalists left them then, turning exhausted horses to pull back up the slope to the inn and the churchyard. They left the sprawled dead and the few wounded of the enemy to the mercy of the townsmen and gathered their own wounded to tend in the inn courtyard where Godolphin lay already dead, a soldier poet to be mourned and remembered even in those urgent days.

Who knows the mysterious separation of the body and the spirit? Francis grieved momentarily for his body that had been so tenderly loved. For a brief and dread moment he saw a reassembling of the faces of the dead, both comrades and enemies, acknowledging in that instant their humanity as his own; their lives stolen as his had been. Then, coming for him, as it had, he realised, even in their moments of terror, come for her and for their son, "A wave o' the sea, that you might ever do nothing but that; move still, still so". And he cast himself freely, lightly, gratefully, into its bright and jewelled surge.

Perhaps, pious and kindly, some might come from the village and give him, and those few others with him, burial. Otherwise they would be left to the fox and the crows and the slow embrace of the earth.

***

In some way, instinctive as the knowledge of weather and the ways of beasts, John became aware that he was masterless as the bitter cold of winter took hold that February. Formal word of Francis' fate would never come. As the farm lapsed into neglect and damp, at home with her relatives in Muchelney, hindered by the impassable winter roads, Francis' stepmother Madeline wondered often whether there would be any news. She believed and hoped that Julia and the child would have taken refuge from the uncertainties of war with Julia's father in Sherborne. But the roads were unsafe for her to travel to find out: the onset of winter had brought, with the darkness, vagrants, deserters and beggars who haunted the lanes and wooded copses. The road to Langport from Muchelney and then on to Sherborne had been churned by the trampling feet of marching men and rutted with the supply wagons and even if it had been safe, it was impassable in the drenching rain. She could gain no news of them. When, long after spring returned, she sent to Sherborne, there was nothing. An old man dead, the daughter and child's whereabouts unknown. One day in May, she went with one of the servants by horse and cart to the farmhouse, only to find it blind and empty. As the war dragged its weary wake of years and she waited for news that never came she would realise slowly, sadly, that Francis also was lost.

From some profound and aching loyalty, John and his wife

had attempted to keep the farm running as October turned to November, but the fields lay unploughed, and the animals wandered and some were lost or stolen beyond the boundary of the farm. John took the remaining animals for sale as the winter fodder ran out and he and Marjory talked of travelling east in the spring to Shaftesbury, where she had a cousin who might know where work would be found. But at the end of February he came home to find her gasping for breath, sweating with fever, calling for him repeatedly: 'John, John, John,' and once, towards dawn, 'Nell!' He held her hand through the night, struggling to cool her forehead and wipe away the sweat entangled hair that had greyed and thinned in these past months. So little trace remained now, in this distress, of the woman he had courted and loved. He urged her to drink what simple remedies he could beg from their neighbours, but as light began to enter the dark, chill room, he watched her eyes blur and dim as she slipped away from him into some place he could not yet follow.

For a little while he lingered after her, begging from village to village, seeking casual labour, to dig or to cut back hedges or mend the holes torn in the roads by the rush of storm water, the ravage of wheels and the passage of cavalry and marching men. He travelled slowly, his body weakened with exhaustion and sorrow, through a despoiled countryside, where the harvest had sometimes been left to rot, sour and sodden in the fields, or the pasture was overgrown and coarse, stripped of livestock by advancing armies. The desolation and the dislocation of its centuries' old patterns of growth and harvest, mirrored his own uprooting and loss, but he held to the memory of love, the certainty of mercy. Words came to him at last as he drifted into sleep in the bitter night cold of late March, though he did not know where they came from. Words of the old parson he guessed and took them and carried them with him as a gift into the chill, gathering, yet welcome darkness. Something of waters, he remembered. Waters, floods, that could never drown love.

***

Left behind them, the locked house with its blank windows was soon filled only with time and dust. When the spring came, beggars and deserters sought shelter in its outbuildings, and then, growing bolder, broke in the door and took what they could carry of clothes and furnishings and what few valuables were left. Hidden and unknown behind the wall in the cellar, the entwined waiting bodies fell slowly into decay, shrinking to bone in the dry air, their hair and clothing separating into sparse fibres; colour and texture diminishing as the years turned to centuries.

Chapter Nine

Amos, Thomas, Will

Theresa could find out so little despite all her research. A possible name, an approximate date, an intuition of the protective love, the madness of grief that had concealed those violated bodies: that was all. What she could not imagine was the aftermath of this violence. The husband she could envisage, riding away to the consuming imperative of war, but what of those who had killed this woman and her child? One man or more than one? And how and why had they come? Did remorse for what they had done shape their lives afterwards, or was this only one among many such acts, pitiless and meaningless, in the surge of war? She found herself thinking of this, placing it alongside what little she knew of her father's wartime experience, and what was now so often in the news: young men posing beside cruelly slaughtered bodies. Then to return, from having seen and perpetrated such things: how could they become again, husband, son, brother? She did not know.

***

Months before Francis, John and Marjory had made their welcome surrender to death, the three young men had lurched away from the farmhouse, leaving behind them a woman and her child fixed forever in an embrace in the cellar; a young girl horribly tumbled in death in the doorway to the barn.

In that past moment, the parents of the girl are stirring even as the three men flee away, and now are finding the humiliated body of their child, and are holding her, soundless, helpless, in their grief. Later, they will go into the house, and see the tracks of damage: the crucifix wrenched from the wall, the table overturned, chests thrust open, cabinet doors swinging and their contents strewn. Boxes that might have held money or jewellery are tipped up and thrown aside. A single lit candle flickers to show them this and then without words they turn, drawn to the door left agape in the kitchen and the steps down to the cellar. John takes the candle and descends. His wife, aged suddenly and trembling, follows him, unable to be parted from him, not because of fear, but in the deep instinctive unity of their lives together. There they find the body of their mistress and her child, bloody, stabbed, fused in death. Their limbs are already stiffening, just as the blood is beginning to turn from the bright crimson of its first effusion to a thin brown glaze. So for John and Marjory now a saving recourse to habits of duty, patterns of devotion. They bring their child in to shelter and lay her on the settle, covering her with cloth. Then they must find Francis and bring him here, to what was his home. In the early chill hours of the morning they set out together.

***

Will, as he runs, sees the darkness and the shadows encroaching on him and hears the hoarse breaths of his companions and his own, labouring as they struggle to set miles of distance between themselves and the horror they have left. The colour of her blood, the child's eyes widening in fear, the shameful abuse of the maid and her pale, limpid face dead beneath him, all of these things are fixed behind his eyes and he feels they will never leave him. He had not imagined death as something near to him. It belonged to the old, to the sick. Not to the young. It belonged to his parents, barely remembered, dead long ago one stifling summer of the plague. Now he had seen it: its suddenness, its incontrovertible finality. And caused it. At least in part. He did not like to think of that moment of panic that had caused him to seize his short sword and stab the child, and through the child, the mother. He did not understand how he had been brought to that moment of proving himself, of taking action, goaded and ridiculed as he had been about his sexual ignorance, his cowardice.

All this, in incoherent spurts of thought and feeling, kept pace with his stumbling feet, running, running through lanes of high hedges and steep banks. The blank dark began to fade and the sky turned to the colour of watery milk with the coming of dawn. Shapes that had loomed over him became recognisable: a tree, a bush, tall seeded grasses. Ahead of him, the others were running on, and he, lost, afraid, had struggled in their wake.

How had they come to this place, he wondered, this act of murderous impulse? All three of them had fled from the siege of Sherborne Castle. Repeated night time firing on the Roundhead positions and then the crack and roar of the Royalist artillery pieces at dead of night that had led so many of them to desert, shaken and frightened by the sounds of destruction and a threat of imminent death. Neither Will nor Thomas knew their way in the darkness, London apprentices who had never, until this present conflict, left city streets. The clouded night, high banked lanes and the brooding silences of the landscape had left them confused as well as afraid. Amos had led them, turning west, skirting the town of Yeovil in a wide detour, persuading them that he knew the countryside and could bring them to where they would be safe and hidden until they could make their way secretly back to London. Safer, he had said then, persuasively, to go west, not east. They would not be searched for if they moved deeper into the countryside. They knew the penalty for desertion if recognised: flogging, perhaps even death. They must hide and then re-make themselves and forget who they were, forget that this had ever happened.

Looking back on the past few hectic days, Will began to understand that fear under the bombardment of the Royalist guns and then desertion had made them ashamed. Days and nights of hiding and hunger compelled them to reassert some kind of manhood, some power over others. Easy to trap and seek to rape a young girl, to knock down her ageing parents. Easy too to break into the home, to steal, to damage, to violate: the mounting excitement, the throbbing fever of it, the sense of sway, of supremacy. And then the pretext: the crucifix on the wall, the likelihood that these were of the king's party, perhaps even adherents of that Papist whore, his wife. That made it so easy: no longer need there be recognition of the vulnerability, the dignity or courage of the mother, the tenderness of the child. They were the enemy. Idolaters. The other. Almost, it made it a necessity to kill them, an act of righteousness. That is how Amos argued, when many stumbled miles further south, they hid in an oak copse high above the surrounding fields, hungry and chilled now that the sweat of running was drying on them.

Thomas was still caught in sudden spasms of giggling laughter, his terror and excitement mingled with shame as he remembered. Amos was calm. But then he had always been so, Will realised. Always the leader, strong and persuasive. A little older than Thomas, three or four years older than himself. He seemed to be unmoved by what they had done. For perhaps a brief hour he had been caught up in the panic that had led them to escape from Sherborne. And for a brief while, he had led their stumbling flight from the scene of their assault at the farmhouse. Now he was steady, clear about what they must do, how they would survive. He had told them that he knew the countryside, having grown up in Yeovil before being sent to a distant relative in London to be apprenticed to a glover, almost seven years ago. That was why they had been convinced to accompany him to enlist in the growing army of the Earl of Bedford, learning together to trail a pike, and growing used to the weight of helmet and corselet, and the handling of a short sword. They were barely tested in conflict, but swaggering in their armour and learning fast how to use the slogans of religion and politics that they had learned in London to gain a place among men who held, perhaps, a simpler, more sincere creed of loyalty.

They had met, the three of them, as apprentices some years before, in the City Trained Band, preparing in those days for a war that no-one would have believed possible. Thomas, apprenticed to a saddler. Himself, to a leather-seller. To run away to war that August, leaving behind the streets of London, fermenting as they would be in the hot weather with disease and crowds and ranting politics and zeal: it had seemed a great adventure. Now they must make their way back through furtive lanes and see how their fortunes could be mended. Will, shocked and terrified by what he had done, knew that he would never be able to follow Amos further in this war. Once he was back in London he would seek out his master, and take the beating that he knew would await him. To run away from an apprenticeship was to be severely punished, but that could be borne. What he could not bear was this torment of soul, this fear that walked with him at every step. He could not enlist again, even though his companions were already talking about how they would seek to be recruited in armies that would campaign in the East or the Midlands. He kept silent about his own plans: secrecy, like linen strips, already tightening its folds around his mind as he knew it must, always.

It took him many days even to begin to piece together the past and the future. His thoughts flinched away from the memories of those minutes, those fragments of time, at the farm. They hid and slept by day and for him, lying awake and listening to the sleeping grunts of his companions, the time passed with terrible slowness. They stumbled through dark lanes, across stubbled fields, beneath the breathing stillness of oak woods by night. Avoiding the streets of villages until they saw all lights extinguished, they crept through, cursing the barking dogs that threatened to expose them. The light would broaden as the sun rose and they would secrete themselves in undergrowth, in abandoned barns, in the tumbledown ruins of old cottages. He spent hours afraid to close his eyes, especially in the early days of their journey for fear that blood would spurt afresh from the images that waited for him. So he was haggard with sleeplessness for the most part, close to his fellows, but far removed from them as they hid, waiting for nightfall. And each slow and sore-footed day they moved east, and became bolder, freer to move at last in daylight.

As they left behind the lanes of Dorset, skirting Shaftesbury, then moving northeast beyond Salisbury, Amos brought them out onto the roads, and his speech broadened to the language of the West Country of his birth and he spun a tale of three young men devoted to the cause of Parliament, determined to reach London and the chance to enlist. Some listened with sympathy, eyeing their ragged clothes and the strips of cloth tied round their feet, and gave them money, enough for ale and bread, even meat. Others turned them away, and some threw stones as they left. They thieved from outlying cottages if they found them empty, and stole from under the feathered rumps of hens. Some days they enjoyed the mildness of late September weather, but on others, chill mist and ceaseless drizzle and then drenching downpours overtook them as autumn moved towards winter.

Amos, so persuasive a leader, was swift to seize whatever opportunities presented themselves to beg or lie, to steal or even pick up casual work for a day. Amos, Will thought, but no longer with admiration. It was as though he was now stripped of a cloak which had invested him with power over them. Because of family connections, they had believed that he would be able to find his way around, gain advantage for them in the West Country. They had been credulous, younger, swayed and stupefied by his rhetoric, his easy confidence, his sexual boasts, his religious fervour. Returning from their training with the City Band he would take them past street women, who would pause, hand on hip, to leer at him as he called them by name and ogled them and pinched them and patted and stroked their breasts, and all the time, they had walked an admiring pace behind him and thought him a man of the world. Perhaps those same women had sneered at his passing, though he knew it not. Nor did Will have eyes to see in those days.

He had never before realised, (and now he struggled to

understand) that Amos was more than one person, nor had Will ever recognised or questioned the disparity of these separate selves. He would take them to hear street preachers and especially to those who mingled religious zeal with political demand, as one and the same. Those who taught equality in the Church, equality in the state, the overthrow of clergy and monarchy together. There he would join in the responses with fervour and passion, becoming unrecognisable to Will. Suddenly, a pale and sweating countenance, with cheekbones that seemed to spring from a face made gaunt with exultation, his breathing hoarse and heavy with devotion. And others, alongside them, some as young as twelve and thirteen, barely out of childhood, apprentices like himself all those years ago. Others were the disaffected, the discontented, workless men and veterans of failed wars, stirring now with an impulse of hate, engulfed in a torrent of words, a dark stream that would lead some to war, not for principle, not for freedoms, but because of the deeply instinctive excitement of violence. And violence that they could cloak with the merits of religion, a covering for all manner of brutality.

Archbishop Laud's Book of Sports. As he stumbled along the lanes, Will suddenly remembered how it had been vilified by preachers and in broadsheets, yet it had offered to some of them, especially apprentices, the very opportunities they longed for. A freedom from restriction, the liberty to enjoy the Sabbath as a time of recreation following devotion. How much more natural for these pinched and pale-faced apprentices to enjoy such emancipation! And yet they hung upon the words that offered them a different permission: the permission to hate, to vilify and condemn those that they judged the servants of the antichrist. There was no need to name the queen's grace, nor the archbishop, now imprisoned by Parliament, whom some now saw as the agent of a return to Rome. The repetitions of hatred: “Papist”, “Antichrist”, “workers of darkness”, “Whore of Rome”. They were caught up, reiterated, gathering at each repetition a fresh intensity, a fresh and unquestioned validity. Boys little more than children ran from such gatherings inflamed with slogans that they did not understand. And so did I, he thought, now sleepless and afraid. Afraid of what had been unleashed in himself. Afraid of his companions. And of the future.

He listened now to the rhythms of Amos’ speech. Phrases that were repeated again and again even in the sparse conversation between themselves, between young men who knew the lies and the slogans for what they were, the mouthings of fanatics. Amos would practise on them the rhythmic, monotonous repetitions of hatred, ‘Engines of Satan; Whore of Babylon, yea, Sword of Righteousness; Tyrant Idolater, yea, Man of Blood...’ The sway and reiteration of the words and phrases compelled, persuaded, even when in his true mind, Will knew that all was false; that this man who held their lives in his hand neither believed these things nor cared; he was enthralled by the power it gave him to hold them in his control. To hold them, and many others to come, Will realised, helplessly. He saw Thomas caught in the web of his words, his mouth slack and wet, his hands plucking, plucking at blades of grass. Sometimes he would still break into a high-pitched bray of laughter and Amos would slap him on the shoulder or grip his wrist to quieten him. He and Thomas would whisper together, and Will, overhearing sometimes, but not included, heard how they were recreating themselves, no longer fugitives, but dedicated supporters of a cause, seeking to enlist where they would not be known, eager young men trained to the pike and short sword and now ready to serve. And they will tell and re-tell their stories until they have new names, new histories to offer to the emerging armies of Parliament. There among the fringe extremes of fanatical Puritanism they will join a chorus of fulmination against the Man of Blood, Charles Stuart and the Antichrist of Rome, and somewhere deep within that madness the murder and desecration of a helpless girl and a young woman and her child would become "spoils of war". All this Will could foresee with dreadful prescience. And more dreadful to him was the knowledge that he would never be free of it: their guilt and indifference had been transferred to him in ways that he did not understand and he must carry it as his burden. Already it bowed his shoulders, wearied his heart. He knew no way of being set free. Perhaps a different creed would have led him to the relief of confession, but the stark teaching, only half understood, that had been so compelling in the months before they had left London, had left him naked before the implacable righteousness of God. He knew, deep within himself that he could have no assurance that he was one of the Elect, no assurance of mercy. There was for him now merely the certainty of being cast into outer darkness. To where there would only be the wailing of the lost. Days, weeks, stumbling exhausted and reluctantly dependent behind Amos and Thomas had scoured his mind, left him devoid of hope. Whatever life he had would be one of pretence. Familiar things would own him again: his master's house and business, the careful road of apprenticeship, the dutiful habits of obedience. Learning to judge the feel and worth of leather between his finger and thumb, the stench of the tanneries, the crowds and restless energy of the city streets, it would be as it had been. Except for this secret, stifling memory, this maggot of guilt. Remorse without repentance; regret without the relief of forgiveness; a secret that could not be confided.

But even as he came with his companions, to within sight of the spires of London churches piercing the brown smoke of the city, he had changed, hardened his mind. Fear had exhausted him, and now he must find ways to survive, fend off that greatest fear of all, the fear of death.

***

It had taken them weeks to return to the familiar streets of the city. Heading steadily east all the time, at first moving mostly by night, they had stolen and begged their way. They were ragged and filthy by the time they returned, and barely speaking to one another. They came across the wide heath of Surrey, twisted with heather roots that snatched and scraped at bloodied feet, and then they tracked through lanes that led them into the darkening chill thickets of the great North Wood. Some days later they came into the borders of Kent, striking east by the pale morning sun to find the road that ran from London Bridge south to Dover. Meeting it, they turned north at last, to struggle wearily and with renewed anxiety through the maze of streets and ditches in Southwark to reach the river. And so to the Thames, churning in its tidal race through the narrow arches of the bridge. Here they would separate. Amos boasted that he could find shelter with one of the women he remembered in the stews and Thomas with him. Will shook his head. He tried to pass it off with a jest, one that he had practised in preparation for this moment.

'I was never made for soldiering,' he said, and shrugged. 'Say what you like, I'm best off selling leather for buff-coats and boots for others to wear, not wearing them myself.' He tried to joke. 'Who knows, in this time of war, there's profit to be made.' Thomas was indifferent, eager to stay with Amos, captivated by him. But Amos looked hard at him, with an intensity of gaze that broke Will's defiance down.

They stood, held rigidly together by the unspoken, the unadmitted events of the past weeks. Amos whispered at last, mouthing hot words close to Will's head. 'There are things that must never be said. You know what I mean. I hold you between my finger and thumb.' He gestured, snapping them in the air, as though Will were a twig and he could break him and toss him aside. 'Never be spoken of. Else I too can speak.'

He continued to stare at him for a moment longer, then turned away with Thomas at his shoulder. They left Will standing by the slimed wooden piles that marked the river's edge, and they did not look back.

Chapter Ten

Will

For a long time, Will leaned against a wall, breathing as though he had been running. The bulk of what had been for centuries, so old folk said, St Mary's Overlie church, now St Saviour's, reached high above him.

But not for me, he thought, *no such saviour for me.*

The gutter that ran down the middle of the lane spewed foul clotted water not far from his feet. He became aware slowly of the multitudinous sounds and sights, the faces, bodies that crowded him. He had not remembered the mingled stink of London, the spices unloaded at the waterside, the markets, the gusts of decay and excrement from the open drains that poured into the Thames. He had forgotten the sweat of bodies and the closeness with which they crowded you, the shouts and jeers of the mob, the grind of wheels, and the assault of sounds that hammered the ears. Those things that had once been the very essence of vigour to a young man of eighteen, that other self who had, not many months but a lifetime ago, abandoned his apprenticeship. He remembered now the breadth of sky, the sharp chill of clean dawn air, the spangle of stars, the scent of grass, remembered them once and then turned from the memory as from a forbidden paradise. So now he yearned that the crowds would engulf him, the press of bodies upon his own would drive from him the sense of self and the raucous voices would crowd away the whispers in his mind and the terrible secrets that he held.

He plodded across the bridge, then jostled his way through the throng to the streets at the head of the bridge that were familiar to him, turning towards Bishopsgate, and to his master's house. Here were the streets that he knew, alleyways that he had run down, carefree once, finding his way to Cheapside to meet with Thomas and then joining him and Amos to walk outside the old city walls to drill with the Trained Bands on Moorfields. He passed near St Helen's church where he had gone with his master and the family on Sundays. And then on rare afternoons of freedom, he would join the excited crowds that gathered to hear the preachers in St Paul's churchyard; the to-and-fro of heckling and fervour defying the established order of priest and people, liturgy and worship, within the great church. It had been another life, another self. He knew what awaited him once he had knocked on the heavy door of his master's house. A beating from which the blood would run and a period of disgrace. But then he hoped his master would be merciful. His wife might plead for him: she had a kindly eye for him, having no son of her own. And his master's daughter, younger than him and soft hearted, might add her pleas.

***

When, in the course of time, Will completed his apprenticeship, he began to prosper, as his master prospered, with the increased trade in leather goods for men at war.

Sometimes he wondered whether the events in the West Country had really happened. Perhaps they were some young man's dream of action. But then, guilt and shame would rake through his heart and for days he would fall silent. Sometimes he feared that loose-mouthed Thomas or Amos might return and all would be exposed. Not so terrible a tale if the armies of Parliament continued to defeat those of the king, but in the swaying fortunes of the war, who could be sure? A journeyman now, skilled in the trade, selecting skins and hides with a practised eye, a yet more practised thumb and finger, knowing by the scent of the leather the process of curing and preparation and what it was worth. He seemed a settled, hard working, reserved young man, a fit husband for Anna, the daughter of the house. Some day in the future he might be admitted to the Guild of Leathersellers, his place in life assured even in these troubled times.

A gentle and courteous man, she had believed Will to be, as he courted her with the growing approval of father and mother. So it surprised his new wife that he should be slurred and stumbling with drink before he came to her and that his entry to her bed and body should be so clumsy and then so violent. She bit her lips to prevent herself from crying out and somehow twisted her body from under him as he slumped over her afterwards, his hoarse groans of effort carrying more than she would ever know of lust long-remembered with shame. He did not speak, but fell away into a stupor of relief. He seemed to be a generous and pleasant man in daylight hours, but at night thereafter he rarely came to her, sometimes sitting up sick and shivering, drinking into the small hours of the dawn before falling asleep alone. She was slow to become pregnant, holding her secret of what felt like failure and disgrace to herself. Both of them walked within yards of one another daily, yet it was as though they were locked into their separate closets of concealment.

When the child was born, he could barely touch it, this little boy, so vulnerable and fragile. The boy's grandparents, proud to see their inheritance held in sure and steady hands, celebrated, and he pretended to do so with them, naming the boy George in honour of his father-in-law. But it was a joyless celebration for him: the vulnerability of the child disturbed him with something like terror. He sought refuge in work: the multitude of orders now coming in to equip what would become a standing army, the army of Parliament, with the thick leather required for the buff-jackets of the cavalry and the wax and tallow-treated boots. An army to be equipped that would soon be fighting in Scotland and then in Ireland. Within a year, almost a decade would have elapsed since that concealed memory of shame, and battles had been fought and a cause lost and a cause won, and a king executed. For him, in the privacy of his home, a wife estranged, a child unknown. Yet he prospered. Their home lacked nothing; his old master had retired and died quite suddenly afterwards and all the trade had come to him, and the business expanded daily. One day he would expect to become an alderman. Yet underneath it all, a flaw of secrecy that had cracked the vessel of his mind and sometimes he feared, even now, that he would be exposed and ruined.

The slow years had passed and he had heard nothing: in the bloody campaigns of the long war, perhaps Thomas and Amos had fallen long ago. Yet beyond all reason, he feared them still. Remembering them, and the murder of an innocent girl and a mother and child, whom he could not call by any names of bigotry that would exculpate him, was like a mass of invisible pressure on his heart. He recalled having heard how in past days heretics had been pressed to death with rocks. Sometimes the weight of his secrets and fears was like those stones. Although if the Commonwealth of Oliver Cromwell continued to rule, his offences would be overlooked, but if the exiled king returned - and there were those who whispered that one day he would - who knows what reckoning might be demanded? He knew no-one whom he could tell, and nowhere to seek forgiveness. Wealthy, respected, of status in the city of London, he lived alone despite wife, child, servants and fellow guildsmen and aldermen. And his wife Anna lived alongside him, watching him, at first with pity and regret and then, as she saw how he turned from the child as well as from her, with gathering bitterness.

Their son, George, growing up in such a home where the distances were vast between his mother and his father and between his father and himself, learned slowly that the expanse that stretched between them could never be crossed. As he grew older, he saw his father's sullen, lonely drinking, late into the evening, heard his shuffling footsteps along the corridor to the room he slept in alone, and in the morning stood at his table dreading the bleared gaze of contempt, the inept blow aimed at him if he was not quick enough in obedience. Neither of them knew how to mend what had been broken long before the boy's birth. Once, years before, standing silently at an open door, Will had seen him as a little child, locked in his mother's embrace, and the piercing memory of his brutal murder of a mother and child, tortured him. He could hardly bear to be in the same room with them during his son's infancy.

So, he grew old long before his time, bloated with drinking, with the need to imbibe thirstily each night until the memory and the guilt were soaked away into vagueness and self-forgetfulness or the thick tears of self-pity. He remained sharp in business by day, until the steady saturation of the nights stifled his mind and he lost sight of the profits that could be made by the contracts for the army of the Commonwealth. Gradually, as the years passed, merchants would learn to deal with his quick son George, once he came of sufficient age to be accounted the heir, and the wealth of the family increased again and as Will grew prematurely old, so he was overlooked. A shadow, slumped in the great chair near the fire, a cup of wine always in his hand and his eyes bloodshot, his mind fuddled, so that he could no longer remember what he must always forget and his slow speech was coarsened with lips made clumsy with drinking. The years moved gradually, inevitably, towards the return of the exiled king.

The son was waiting in readiness, confident and shrewd beyond his years, eager for profit, sharp and flexible. Attuned to the rumours of new days and new men in favour, and fashions changing to soft leathers and indulgence, he readied himself and his stock to greet the monarchy's return. The austerity of the Commonwealth gave way to the fervour of celebration, bringing new demands for luxury goods and George, shrewd, responsive, prospered. And Will's wife Anna, who had waited and watched through the years the sluggish decline of her husband, now saw her son supplant him. It was a kind of domestic revenge that eased her bitterness a little, especially when she saw how her adored son George had long since grown to loathe him. A sagging figure in the corner, lost to himself as well as to them, Will slowly passed unnoticed from their lives, and was daily forgotten. Only his death, and thereby the inheritance of a prosperous business, gave him any significance.

Chapter Eleven

Amos, Thomas

After they had parted from Will, late in October, 1642, Thomas and Amos slid sideways into the labyrinth of narrow streets and ponds that were entwined together on the south side of the Thames, to seek out the whores and cutpurses that Amos claimed to know. There, Amos boasted, they would find shelter for the night, different clothes in which to disguise themselves, and the means to escape all recognition in London and enlist in the armies of the Eastern Association. The ranks of my Lord of Essex, or the newly recognised Colonel Cromwell, whose name was on all lips. Either, as long as there would be fighting and the pickings that attended it. The pious mouthings Amos constantly rehearsed with Thomas would be their passport to acceptance. Amos' ready tongue, telling their story of suffering and escape from the West Country and a long, footsore and perilous journey back to London, won them sympathy, food and squalid lodging for the night.

In the morning they haggled for a change of clothes, barely less ragged than the clothes they had worn on their travels, but at least with hoods that could be pulled over their heads. Very early they joined the crowd of carters and shop boys, market women and servants that jostled for position on the bridge. They crossed the racing Thames, that surged thickly through the piers of the bridge as it forced its way upstream with the incoming tide. They avoided familiar streets, lest they should be identified by some wide awake apprentice, and turned east, skirting the huge grim walls of the Tower, and then northeast, to seek the road towards Huntingdon. They aimed to reach more than twelve miles beyond the city before nightfall, where they might know themselves to be free of pursuit or recognition by any. Then to beg if need be, but more often to persuade the credulous of their devotion to the cause, to be sent on their way with a blessing, a meal, sometimes a pair of shoes or a coat. And so they made their way, Amos, convincing even himself with his zeal, Thomas submissive to him, fascinated, docile.

As foot soldiers, shouldering pikes as well as pack and short sword, they learned the drill of a more disciplined army and marched the weary miles of campaigning that took them the length of England for the years of the decade. Amos and Thomas saw the war in all its sad and wasteful horror, yet remained unmoved. They joined with wanton glee in the wreckage of churches, the high reaching windows shattered by well-aimed stones, so that the ancient watchful faces of saint and prophet, Virgin and Infant, fell in shards of red and gold and blue onto the stone floors. Altars were dragged into the centre of the church and overthrown, and their rails and screens torn out for firewood. Blackened stains of fire on the stone slabs of the nave marked their ruin. Or on other cold nights of pelting rain, the horses were brought in for shelter alongside the men and their dung and stained straw were left to defile the sanctuary. And in their departing wake, the carved traceries of chancels, the wings of angels, the faces of saints, were clubbed and smashed. At other times they participated in the sack of garrisons, and in reprisal for their resistance, the slaughter of prisoners and the plundering of goods and sometimes, secretly, though not in isolation, the abuse of women. It had become a necessary violence, each act obliterating the one before, creating a hunger for the next.

Both preserved the bearing of staunch Puritans, stern and devout, with a seeming devotion to the cause that brought each of them into the close knit ranks of the most zealous, the most trusted, earning for themselves approval and for Amos, promotion to sergeant, and the halberd of his rank. Both he and Thomas had found a place in the New Model Army and, as volunteers, were eagerly accepted at a time when Parliament was resorting to impressment. Amos had hidden himself among them, so perfectly concealed that he himself had forgotten that this was ever a disguise. Men followed him, men of sincerity and faith, of devout worship, magnetised by his fervour, by his headlong courage in battle, by the intensity of his stark eyes and hoarse, repetitive voice. He had learned almost by instinct how powerful is the iteration of zeal: how easily men may mistake the concealed hatred of difference for the expressed yearning for an untainted righteousness, and how that envious hatred can then destroy beauty, craftsmanship and art, and even laughter, in its pursuit of purity.

***

Somehow on that September night, now many years ago, a casement had been slammed shut in Thomas' mind. An immature and dependent young man of nineteen was now bonded with Amos as a blind man is to the hand that leads; a beggar to the voice that is kind. Sometimes darkness and memory seeped into his mind with some shred of regret, of conscience or kindliness that would, if unchecked, cause him to shake, to break into high-pitched barks of laughter. Then Amos would quiet him with repetitions of fervour, watchwords of vengeance, culled from preachers who themselves spoke with the vehemence of apocalyptic visions.

Sometimes men envied the seemingly favoured position Thomas held with their sergeant, but Amos would turn and shrug and say to them, 'Long companions through this vale of tears, yea, on these battle plains of Armageddon. This man, yea, the sword of the Lord,' and they might mutter amongst themselves, but dared not confront or question. And when they saw Thomas fighting, no-one could challenge his courage or his devotion. But Amos knew that his mind hung by a thread.

Amos had lost all awareness of whether he believed or not: it no longer mattered to him even to pretend to examine himself. Among the ranks of the army were men of devotion and purity of faith, but he was untouched by their sincerity, their simplicity of doctrine. The chanted watchwords of religion, the call for freedom from the man they called a Tyrant, a Man of Blood, had become for him and for Thomas, as for many, a fervency of repetition. It carried its own intense compulsion, consuming, yet at the same time fuelling the mind and the will. A trail of violence stretched behind them both, legitimised as deeds of war, but secretly, privately, an insatiable lust, a need to numb all senses, all memory, all sensibility, with successive acts of blood.

Thomas fell at last at the battle of Naseby, in June, 1645, surprised perhaps by his own transience and the inability of his friend to save him. His eyes widened in the bewilderment of encroaching death and his mouth fell slack with the agony of the musket ball that had taken him in the stomach. He lay piteously for many minutes, cold and alone, writhing as he bled to death and crying out for the man he thought was his friend. And Amos strode heedlessly away from him, to join the pillaging of the king's baggage train, and the slaughter of women, camp-followers, declared to be Irish and therefore undeserving of quarter, before marshalling his company to escort the humiliated and weary Royalist prisoners of war to London. In the ensuing four years of war, Amos played a careful hand, relieved of a burden that had been a perilous one; a dependent that might at any moment stray into a hysteric admission of those secrets that bound them together. He steered now between the extremes of political and religious opinion and attached himself by instinct to Cromwell, whose military skill, political ruthlessness and influence were to see the king brought at last to trial on charges of High Treason.

On a bitterly chill day in January, 1649, Charles stepped out upon the platform that had been raised for his execution. From his oval face, white, extraordinarily dignified, his calm eyes gazed out upon a shocked and silent crowd, before he knelt at the block and his head was severed from his body. Amos, halberd of his rank unwavering in his right hand, was amongst the soldiers of the guard that surrounded the scaffold.

***

Cromwell's authority secured Amos' rank and future. Following his commander-in-chief to campaign in Scotland and against the army of the Scots which had invaded England in Charles the Second's disastrous bid to recapture his kingdom, he was battle-hardened, as if a carapace of immunity protected him from any sense of fear or pity or remorse. The events seven years before in a remote farmhouse in Somerset were long eclipsed, justified then by the reiteration of bigotry and forgotten now in the welter of violence and cruelty that had been let loose in nearly a decade of wasteful Civil War. So, at last, his long path brought him, in August 1649, to Ireland, to cross the Irish Sea with sea-sick men and terrified cavalry horses, with the intent to disembark near Dublin. Cromwell had been sent by Parliament with clear orders: to march on garrisons of resistance to crush fears of a Royalist and Catholic invasion to be launched from Ireland in support of the newly declared King Charles the Second. Yet more compelling and inflammatory amongst many of the soldiers, Amos among them, was the catchphrase that this was a righteous act of vengeance for the massacre of Protestants believed to have been conducted by the Irish eight years before.

But for Amos, even the fixed and ruthless nature of his disciplined soldiery was subdued on that voyage across the Irish Sea. Subdued to the point of weakness by the scream of horses, thrashing below in the hold and by the groaning, cursing men, himself among them, who crouched shivering over the ship's side. Sea sickness consumed him with its dreadful despair of ceaseless vomit and lurching footholds, stench and spray, and human helplessness in the interminable grip of the waves. Waves that slogged against the sides of the ship and cross currents that rolled her sideways to stagger from crest to crest; green, grey and then black as the night drew on. Moments of vulnerability and then of insistent memory broke in on him in engulfing self-pity: a small boy, fatherless, and a weak and demanding sister. Tormenting her because of his envious hatred of the attention she stole from his mother. Unmanageable at home, he had been sent, too young at twelve, to be an apprentice to London merchants, distant relations of his mother, the Glovers. He remembered learning at first how to dodge the blows of the older apprentice who bullied him, and to run swiftly to meet the impatient demands of his masters. The other servants mocked him, his broad accent, his country ways. So Amos had learned to make his way, first by fist fighting and kicking. Then winning, by lies and deceit and by the power of cruel language and cleverness, until one day he realised his dominance over others. Realised the alchemy of repetition and rhythm, the magnetism of his persuasiveness, the compelling energy of his speech and passion. Finding a creed, a cause, that fuelled him, now gave him justifications that he almost believed. Even now, spewing and shaking in an ague of wretchedness, he knew his power, knew that men feared him. On dry land, no-one would dare say that they had seen him weakened as they had been weakened. He spat out the bile, wiped his hand across his mouth, smelling the sour stink of himself, and turned, forcing himself to stand straighter, to hold hard to the ropes that stretched by him and stare out over the dark tumult of the waves. He found a foothold on the sliding deck from which to ride them, to defy them, remembering how London boatmen defied the race that ran thick and churning between the piers of the great London Bridge and how they had learned to laugh at the violence that could dash their boats and themselves to splinters against its stone.

He came ashore at last with the great army that disembarked, all of them, man and horse alike, weakened with the voyage and now facing the twenty miles or more that must be marched north to besiege the walls and the garrison of Drogheda. The weather was stormy and unpredictable, an August of unrelenting, saturating rain, and conditions of disease and misery already gripped and weakened the ranks of the army in a hostile country. Sickness and hunger were depleting the resources that Cromwell could count on and the campaigning season was drawing towards its end. But then, at last, the necessary reinforcements arrived and the army gathered itself, north of Dublin, horse, foot and artillery, to move steadily forward. The great siege guns, waiting to be heaved by rolling-eyed horses on the drenched and rutted roads would be brought up in readiness to blast down the walls, and the infantry, Amos among them, deployed to follow through into the breaches made.

The sodden days had turned to September and the imminence of an unpredictable autumn in the campaigning season. The army was at last grouped in readiness before the walls of Drogheda and a formal demand for surrender was made to the commander of the garrison. That being refused, the guns began that evening their pounding work of destruction. The next day they were readied to renew with ferocity their battery of the east and south walls adjoining St Mary's church, and so enable the foot soldiers to storm the gaping holes made in the masonry and gain the advantage of that position.

Amidst the tumbling masonry and thick, swirling dust, the infantry encountered fierce and wild resistance, pressing their attack forward at the cost of many lives to take the town. Here men of Amos' company fell, slithering on the broken, blood-slimed stones as musket ball and sword thrust caught them. And now he too fell among them, choking on the blood that bubbled from a pierced lung, and was trampled on in the sway and thrust of hand to hand, breast to breast fighting. If any had paused to see his last, grasping moments of life, they might have recognised that his careful mask had slipped. His fixed and staring eyes conceded now the shocking affront of his shared mortality and then, at last, the horror of death.

It was the 10th September, 1649. A day of losses and brutal victory. Amos had been cut down and now lay askew, strewn in the threshing of death with others of his company. Each one, battered and bloody, stripped of weapons, boots and shoes, leather jackets, all of value, was tumbled into an Irish ditch for burial with his fellows, under the earnest prayers of the chaplain.

***

So severe had been the resistance to his army that once the town was taken, Cromwell gave the order that no mercy should be shown to any who had been taken in arms: one tenth to be executed, the rest shipped to Barbados. And among the dead, killed in the zealous compulsion of battle and vengeance, unarmed priests and friars.

Cromwell, that complex man of courage and fervour, ruthlessness and implacable conviction, oscillating now between the mercy of God and the brutality of man, stained his reputation and marred the memories of a nation by an impulse of reprisal. And gave yet more cause for future generations to revile his name by the record he made in his letter to the Speaker of the House of Parliament, some seven days later. A consuming fire of unquestioning righteousness burned in him, yet also a compelling need to justify to himself and to others the actions of the campaign. So, dipping his sharpened quill pen into gall-ground ink, he scratched his report.

'I am persuaded that this is a righteous judgment of God upon these barbarous wretches, who have imbrued their hands in so much innocent blood; and that it will tend to prevent the effusion of blood for the future. Which are the satisfactory grounds to such actions, which otherwise cannot but work remorse and regret.'

So much innocent blood.

Chapter Twelve

Theresa, Tony, Adam

The coming of summer had brought healing to the Levels, as it had through countless centuries' past cycles of devastation and recovery. Yet its progress was slow to the flood-wearied people and to their homes and livelihoods. Bloated fields of mud and ruin slowly drained to reveal sharp blades of living green again and the roads were mended. The rhynes were scoured for drainage, and the rivers dredged. Promises of flood prevention and what was called "an emerging vision for the future" drew Theresa into community action groups and she and Adam worked with new-found neighbours to clear the debris that clogged the waterways and drag away for removal the strange silted wreckage that lay stranded, upended at the edge of roads and ditches as the water receded. Drowned cars and bicycles, buggies and sodden televisions, horribly rotted creatures, disjointed furniture. Alongside the cleansed waters, she saw re-emerging the ancient pattern of life: a rich and varied pasture, criss-crossed by rhynes, their lines of pollard willow distinct against the pale, translucent evening light of August and September. At first, Adam was hesitant, uncertain in this endless open landscape of greenness and silver water, that glanced with light and cloud shadow. But then he walked with growing confidence in the fields near to their home, observing the changing skies, and, book in hand, learning to name the vibrant meadow flowers, the settling flocks of birds and the water birds that dabbed and strutted along the ditches. Towards the end of August, lapwings returned, their green backs metallic in the glinting sun. In September, the gabbling voices of geese drew Theresa and Adam outside to watch the trailing threads of their flight across the evening skies.

Sometimes they would drive together, taking food to share, exploring this land that was both new and somehow home to them. They found, towards the end of one still afternoon, the quiet of Muchelney Abbey and the ageless endurance of its stone walls: ruined yet indestructibly a place of restoration. They also came to love Sherborne, and visited frequently, to shop, but also to meander: the old castle, the streets of honeyed stone, the school glimpsed beside the abbey and the abbey itself. They wandered in often, standing to gaze in stillness at the arched glory of the abbey ceiling with its high branching traceries of carvings and the colours of the stained glass windows that splashed vibrant onto the paving in the afternoon sun.

In those September evenings, as the days began to shorten, Theresa found herself reflecting on the past, at once so immediate and yet now so distant. What path had brought her here? She remembered watching, through the oblong medium of the television screen, so safely remote in their London home, the waters rising, lapping at the edges of fields before swallowing them, engulfing roads and hedges. Headline news, for a matter of days, until superseded by other events: the gathering horror of attacks in Iraq, in Syria, in Libya; a lone schoolboy gunman killing his fellow students in a Moscow school. The immediacy of such violence and brokenness had crowded out the silent images of the rising waters, pewter under pale skies, stealthily and inexorably drowning the land. Images of abandoned cars, farms islanded by flood, roads that could be traced only by the jagged lines of hedge, or the upraised hands of trees. She had dreaded the destruction of this house, slowly realising that in a working life of buying and selling property, and a succession of houses they had called home, this place alone had become vital to her. She had known even then that her own concern was selfish, detached from others' genuine loss of home and livelihood. She forced herself to be honest about that. To recognise that her life had been, in so many respects, shielded, screened from what was harsh or anguished. Only in the struggle to protect and support her son had she pierced the careful protection afforded by wealth and the comforts it had brought to them all.

She saw quite clearly now, her careful preservation of herself, recognising all her past defences against age, against loss of looks or poise. Success and its accompanying prosperity had come at the cost of her secret, hidden insecurities. They had moved home to enter neighbourhoods where she had hidden their origins, driven like others to join the waiting cars outside the preparatory schools, enrolled her daughters in classes for music, tap and ballet, and later for the tutorials that would secure their place at private schools and university. There had not been time to admit to herself her essential loneliness. But now and here, as the waters drained, and the miracle of returning spring and then summer had brought an extraordinary vivid greening to the land, she knew a renewal in herself. In the old story of the Flood, she remembered a dove had been sent out. And a raven. She was not clear about the details, but it had been the dove that had returned, of that she was sure. And had returned with evidence of life in its beak. That was how it felt for her.

The past had laid its hand on her, but not with death or diminishing. Past lives that had been lived simply, in love and vulnerability, had left their impression on the present, as they would on the future, as a seal in melted wax. Now she realised how little she had understood, even of her own parents' efforts to survive in the years of that war that had defined their time. Walking, gardening, decorating; whenever her mind was set free because the task or the exercise was rhythmic and undemanding, she found herself thinking, stretching out beyond the familiar towards understanding. She had been born long after the war, and of a marriage that struggled daily with the unspoken and unspeakable distances that had grown between her parents since her father's return from Germany. She had been a subdued, careful child. Uncertain always of her place and worth. Earnestly attentive at school, bright but never seeing herself as 'academic'; shy and cautious in the playground and in the games that hopscotched and skipped and alley, alley-o'd in the twilight streets. She remembered vividly, as though the touch had still lingered on her skin, leaning against her father's knee and his hand stroking the hair from her forehead and then falling listlessly from her to hang over the edge of the arm of the chair as though there were no life, no energy left in him, when he came home from work. An office job, somewhere, mysteriously, up the shining, static crackling railway lines to the City. In the evenings they would listen to the wireless together, and her mother would put aside her apron and take up the sewing, and sometimes the shared laughter of "Around the Horn" or "Take it from Here", laughter that she barely understood, would release them, and she could glimpse the young people whose shy, smiling wedding photograph still stood on their mantelpiece. And indeed, she realised, they were not old, even then. Just worn out. Her father had returned from a war that he could not speak of and sights that she only later learned were of utter devastation and brutality. Her mother had grown weary with long fearful waiting and the bombing, and then the rationing. Only now could she really begin to comprehend, and feel the pity of it.

The night before her wedding, her mother had tried to speak, to talk of things that were never mentioned between them. 'Your father,' she had said, hesitant, awkward. 'He was never the same when he came home. Never. Sometimes he could not bear to touch me. Or you. He had seen things. In Germany. Too many bodies, he said, like skeletons. Women and children. Thrown into pits.' Theresa, twenty years old, and almost ignorant of what she meant, found that she was comforting her mother, hushing her as she cried. She struggled to manage a distress so huge that it frightened her. And then her mother held herself a little apart, and wiped the tears with the back of her hand, and apologised. 'Tomorrow is your day,' she said. 'And here am I spoiling it. It's all a long time ago.' Now, glimpsing images in black and white photographs and newsreel, she saw what her mother must have meant, what her father had seen, perhaps handled, in the charnel house of Europe. They never spoke of it again until the last weeks of her mother's life, and then it had seemed too late to find one another.

The next day she had married and all was excitement and happiness and yet the arm of her father shook beneath her hand, she remembered, as she walked with him up the aisle. And Tom had swept her up and she had never looked back, not in the early days of marriage when they had been so caught up in the business, and then as the girls had come. Her father had died, not long after, months, almost a year after her wedding, but no longer, and they had never really spoken. Not even then when she had sat beside him, summoned by her mother's telephone call late one evening, tongue-tied and saddened, as though he were a stranger.

For a while she knew that her mother had enjoyed the grandchildren, and she had welcomed her into their lives, but then she and Tom had become more affluent as the business expanded. They had moved into a better area and the children were sent to private schools and had tutors and music lessons, so almost unnoticeably Theresa's mother had stayed away and faded out of their lives. Her tired life had simply shrunk out of sight, and her death had barely rippled the sheen of their existence. Only now could Theresa admit it, all of it: her parents' labours and sorrow, her own regretful grief, into her thoughts and heart. This strange season of discovery, of renewal, was full of both healing and anguish.

She thought of Adam. At fifteen he had been adrift after the disaster of his schooling. She had found him a tutor and a place at college where he could just cope with the English and the Maths that would be enough for his future. Now, far from London and settled here, she watched him come to life: learning, exploring in ever-widening circles of confidence, working with assurance to restore a garden, finding joy - that was the word that sprang to her mind - in this home, this meeting place of water, sky, earth. Here it must be her aim to give him space to grow, to find himself, to come to a place where he no longer needed her and could seek other relationships and take this house as his own. Perhaps too, before that time came, she would have a chance to offer this home to her daughters to come to visit them. She might be able to get to know them as adults in ways that she had never known them as they had been growing up. There was unspoken healing needed in their relationship with Adam: the un-admitted envy, perhaps of the place he had taken in her life and her all too ready release of them into independence. In the new clarity of her thoughts it seemed to her urgent that she should offer them a renewed relationship, a reconnection with him, as well as with herself.

***

Early that autumn they began to break open the ground in their garden before the frosts would come, to prepare for the planting of a small orchard. Working together at the back of the house they had discovered the ruined footings of a south facing wall and one old and crooked stump and the half rotted roots of what might once have been an apple tree, they guessed. Perhaps it had been planted to be trained to bear fruit, or so she liked to imagine, by that woman who had lain hidden for so long. An orchard created for her child and children's children. The dream of trees that would mature and fruit long after their planting. Now she and her son would plant again, for Adam and for his children's children. They visited the nurseries locally, and Adam listened and learned the names of trees, the best planting season, the waiting time for fruit and he began to read about ways to prune and train, and to talk to the nurserymen when they returned to discuss the merits of fan and espalier.

Towards the end of October, they had the long-awaited call from their insurers. Tom had doubtless been active on their behalf to ensure that the policy was up to date, and at last the surveyor rang to make the appointment to inspect the repair work and assess the safety of the cellar and the foundations. She knew that the Acrow props would be removed once the essential structure was declared safe. The wall that the flood had demolished had not been a load bearing wall, but a single course of bricks between the two stronger columns at the sides. Hastily thrown up, by the look of the rough and clumsily finished lime mortar that was still clinging to some of the stones and bricks where they still lay undisturbed, it had tumbled just as the water had eroded the footings and brought them down. She found herself wondering often whether it been shame or protection that had hidden that entwined casket of bones from view, yet her awakened instincts told her with increasing certainty that it must have been done from love. Some kind of desperate love perhaps, that would seek to hide those bodies. Love that was maddened with loss. Soon all the evidence of it would be cleared away and the cellar would be dry and lit and spacious and its story lost. A broken locket would be labelled and displayed in the museum at Sherborne. Maybe a footnote in a local history booklet. That was all.

Yet all our lives are tangled together, she had thought to herself one day, as she had been looking from a footbridge into the streaming waterweed that wavered beneath her. The past, known and unknown, and the future, and this present time. And what we do now, in this moment.

***

On the last Monday of the month, around two o'clock, the surveyor came, bringing with him a tall young man and introducing him as the intern at the firm, joining them in order to work towards his qualifications as a chartered surveyor.

'This is Tony Skinner,' he had said, introducing him

carefully to Theresa. 'My assistant, serving his internship with us this year. And I am Graham Walker.'

Theresa shook his hand, and turned to his assistant, who seemed not to notice her offered hand, focusing instead on his notebook and calculations. Shy perhaps, she thought, recognising that her own son had difficulties in social situations and retreated from them into task and formality. She excused him in her mind on that account. She noticed his face and hands, brown with the sun, as if he had been abroad for some months in a region of light and warmth.

The surveyor was old and experienced, precise, polite, over-meticulous perhaps. He was it seemed to her, proud of the young man's achievements, which he told her of: the excellent degree, the months spent abroad on voluntary service. Now he took a fatherly, fussily careful interest in him, showing him the limitations of the damage outside the building and then describing the stealthy inroad of the flood into the cellar and the remedial steps taken to ensure that the farmhouse was sufficiently underpinned. They viewed the RSJ that had been put in place beneath the main staircase and then they descended to the cellar, to see the props that he trusted would now be demonstrably unnecessary.

They both followed her through the cellar door, the young man, Tony, needing to bend his head to stoop beneath the low arched supports of the roof.

She waited while they talked and measured, checked and confirmed, and then found herself speaking. 'Here is where we found her, and the child.' She gestured to the dark end of the cellar, where there was a raised shelf of local stone that must have been designed to hold jars or storage casks long ago. The central light could barely reach so far. Once again, strong blades of torch light severed the darkness, flickering on the far wall as they turned to follow her words. In front of the shelf, the as yet uncleared rubble showed where the waters had eroded the crude lime mortar of that single course of stone and bricks, now only partially left standing. At the edge, towards the walls, it was still waist high, but had cracked and scattered at the centre to expose the secret it had protected for so long. She found that she had moved closer to that wall now, ahead of the men, as though she wished to conserve a lingering dust with reverence and breathe the calm, cool air as if it still held their breath. So soon, this damage would be repaired. The traces lost. She thought to herself, urgently, disjointedly, *Love is at the roots of this house. She was attacked and died to protect the child, I am sure of it. Buried with love. Waiting.* She could not understand why she felt such intensity, almost panic, driving her thoughts. And then her mind ran on. *I will restore the cool shelves of this place. I like to think that she would have stored her preserves here as I will. Jars of fruit, dried herbs. They loved this place, made it a home. Whoever buried her did not thrust her out of sight. It was a chosen place.*

'She held the child in her arms. We found them here, an arc of yellowed bones. The child's ribcage fallen within the mother's as though into her womb again.' She could not think what compelled her to speak, to tell with more intimacy than she had ever done before. It was to the young man that she spoke, she realised. Graham Walker nodded with patient, detached kindness, but not the young man, who turned from her. Maybe, she thought, quickly absolving him, he is not used to such immediacy in a woman, a woman who is a stranger. Then the older man excused himself to wander out of the cellar as his phone lit and jangled, pointing to those areas that needed to be carefully measured, checked and recorded and leaving the younger man with her.

'They told us that the blow that killed the child stabbed her too, so that they fell together, here perhaps or nearby. And someone placed them on that shelf and then hid them behind that rough wall where they lay. The floods washed away the footings and the wall collapsed and they were there, visible after more than three centuries.' She could not stop herself repeating the memory, the rushed, simplistic words that still held that first glimpse of those scoured, robbed lives. She paused then, loaded with the pity of it, that spark of agony that had leapt from those long-forgotten bodies to herself when she had seen them. 'I think of her often,' she said quietly, almost to herself. 'And of her child.'

The young man leaned against the wall, not crossing the pile of collapsed brick, and turned on her the bore of dark, levelled eyes as she spoke. 'You stupid, stupid bitch,' he said, silently, contemptuously within his mind. 'I have seen and done worse than this. Who are you to feel pity for the long-dead?' His rage thrust towards her as she touched and roused some crushed denial of feeling within him. Rage so violent: against her, against himself. That she should dare recall him to the infinite pity of one such death! One woman, one child, forever buried in a hollowed plea for compassion. Such rage was directed towards her, that she must surely feel it like a gust of air, stirring the silted rubbish of this human sett. Surely she would feel it jolt against her certainties, her conventional, sentimental feelings?

He looked at her now, not engaging with her eyes, but glancing at her face and form: the hair that she had now allowed to turn grey and escape from the comb that held it up in wisps that she sometimes smoothed back from her forehead and temples. The edges and roots that showed that where there had once been vanity, now there was carelessness. He looked at her: tired, aging, he realised, even as he scorned her for the exposure of her face, her greying hair, her naked forearms. Her offered touch that he had rejected. She turned to him, her face questioning, gentle, sensing, but not understanding, the implacable strength of spirit set against hers. She brought to him a new and terrible awakening to a distinct grief, an individual's sorrow. His generalised hatreds and huge justifications for death might not survive this one, particular, unknown grief. An aging woman moved to tears by telling of a murdered woman, curved in death around the body of her child. "What's Hecuba to him or he to Hecuba?" surfaced in his mind like a bubble breaking through ooze, rising up from long-forgotten lessons in the yawning classrooms of his sixth form college. For a perilous moment he re-inhabited himself, slouched across the grey-topped table. It was sticky beneath the touch of his fingers, stained, scrawled and scratched in the corners. He wondered what possible connection had been made to bring this back to his thoughts, the words as sharp as if they were still being spoken within his head.

Cast back to that time, he watched his pen rolling gently backwards and forwards across the blank sheet of paper, pushed and retracted by one finger. Enrichment classes. That's what they called them. Dust motes stirred and drifted in random gyrations in the slanting winter sunlight. 'The irrational yet vital universal sympathies,' the teacher had said, passionately, to a heedless audience of sixth form students. He must have heard it, because it had lodged in his head and played out now, whether he wanted it or not. 'Despite the artifice of form that Shakespeare is caricaturing, to contrast with what he establishes as Hamlet's reality, true feeling must break through. "What's Hecuba to him, or he to Hecuba?" The irrational yet vital universal sympathies.' If he could, he would erase the memory and spit the words out of his mind.

Now he could not look into that dark space behind the crumbled wall. Nor at the woman, who stood so gently beside it, apologising for her sudden tears and smiling through them at him.

***

Tony had not realised, nor could he, how easily they had recognised his susceptibility to recruitment as they had watched him during his years at university. From the beginning, in Freshers' Week, as the new intake floundered, experimented, stabilised or faltered, they were swift to scrutinise him, and others. They identified his contempt for the girls with whom he had had brief, snatched relationships, encounters in which he stole the sexual submission that he craved, and they saw his swift and ruthless severance from them. They saw his secretly obsessional patterns of behaviour that kept him bound to routines: small, meticulous and disciplined. The notebook always to the left, the pens set in line together, in the lecture theatre. The daily visits to the gym and ever more demanding targets of rigorous endurance. Patterns of self-discipline which were harnessed to a driving ambition. They noted this, as they noted his isolation.

Over the three years of his course, he sought out a variety of religious experience, requiring an ever more compelling rigidity of practice to satisfy his hunger for perfectionism, a purity which could never be satisfied. It was not difficult to draw him further and further in. Disciplined devotion; a brotherhood that assuaged his unacknowledged thirst for love; the lure of promised, gratifying power; the compelling nature of asceticism: all drew him, taking him far beyond the generous practice of the believers who had welcomed him at first, drawing him deep into an austere and secret, excluding, dedicated cadre. Now he was promised the perfection that he craved, a world resolved of all ambiguities, of righteousness that satisfied by its rigid conformity, its uniformity of laws and practice. And although he did not recognise it, he absorbed the compulsion of promised power and dominance; the subjection or destruction of all that deviated from that burning path of purity. Power based on the assertion of a moral superiority; permission to view all else as inferior and apostate and ultimately, less than human. To be eradicated.

He told them little of himself, but enough. He did not allow himself to remember the happiness of his early childhood. Stamped down in his mind for so long, he could no longer recall the boy he once was, laughing with delight as his mother, Karen, pushed him on the swing. Nor how she carried him home on tired shoulders, or took him hand in hand to the nursery school and waited always for him to run across the playground and fling himself into her welcome as she bent to hug him tightly at the end of each day. There were grandparents too, but detached and formal, and he was never sure of their love. It had always been him, and his mother, and an unquestioning intimacy, a sufficiency, a consuming fierce focus of love. But he did remember the day he had first asked her the question that had gradually surfaced in his mind as he began to see more clearly the variation of others' lives around him.

'Where's my dad?' he had asked. Simply, unexpectedly, without preface.

And she had turned in the small kitchen, and looked at him, her face draining away into slanted planes of cheekbone and chin so that she became for a moment a stranger. 'He doesn't live with us,' she said, dully. 'He never has. He went away and never came back.'

Somehow he knew better than to ask why, perhaps fearing in those days that the answer might be that his father went away because he did not love him. He kept the secret of his question hidden, even from himself, and slowly that evening his mother's face returned to her, and she smiled and helped him with his reading, and all was as it had been.

The secret slept until another time. Years, in fact. Until he was tripped by the threshold of adolescence and suddenly the question was imminent, part of his own irresistible sexual awakening, part of the knowledge that came to him out of secret night time arousals and gratification, the thunder of his own pulse compelling him.

'My father,' he said to her, formally, awkwardly, one evening as he came into the kitchen from his room. 'My father. I know he's never lived with us. But I want to know who he was. And why he didn't stay with you.' Already, the words had become words of implied blame.

His mother was in the kitchen of their small flat. Her own work, as a teaching assistant in a primary school, was on the table. She was preparing materials to help children understand numbers, counting, adding and subtracting, he thought, as his eyes flicked over the cards and colours that she was organising for a lesson tomorrow. She looked up as he came in, smiling to hear his feet approaching, but as he entered and his questions thrust in with him, she paused, locked for a breath-held moment, while she sought how to answer him. She saw how he had changed in these last months. Taller, yet less coordinated, as though his limbs and hands and feet did not quite connect as they once had. His voice, shunting from childhood's easy fluency through unpredictable shifts of tone and volume. As best she could, she must be truthful with him.

How do you explain to a boy just out of childhood, the recklessness of passion in the days of its first awakening? Explain it even to herself, flung headlong from a girls' private school into those first weeks of university experience? How can you describe that it felt to her then like an awakening to a sun so brilliant that it blinded her to everything except the compulsion of each moment? Consuming her, demanding the sacrifice of herself to someone of such aloofness and yet passionate intensity that she was enthralled. She wondered now, how many others had been enchanted by him? He, a postgraduate student, completing his engineering project and thesis, soon to return to his home country. She, just nineteen years old, and falling pregnant in that first term. When she knew for certain that she was pregnant she decided to leave the course, already aware that his interest in her had fallen away, long before she had said to him that she might be carrying his child. He had left, and there was no word from him, nor any means of reaching him. Somehow, her parents had helped her to cope, but their disappointment had been hard to disguise and she had been ill at ease with them. So she had struggled to find work, to give him a home, this adored son of hers. Now he was asking for his father. And what could she tell him?

'I was at university,' she began, tentatively. 'I had just started - my first term. I had never been away from home before.' He was listening, the sharp movement of his throat showing that he was swallowing hard, as if trying to gulp down what she was saying. His hands were shoved deep into his pockets, the skin over the bridge of his nose stretched white, his lips tight and straight. She paused, to gather words together. 'I met a young man. He was a postgraduate student, finishing his research and - he was from the Middle East.' She realised that he had never been specific, painting a hypnotic picture of the ancient ruins and unsearchable sands of his land, but never naming it, never giving her a place where she could find him.

'I fell in love, or thought I had fallen in love. I was caught up with him.' She frowned as she tried to explain, allowed herself to remember the heady wildness and destruction. 'Like a moth and a flame.' She struggled to express the torment of the days, the falling, drowning sweetness of them. 'Like a moth,' she repeated. 'I thought I was pregnant just before the end of term, but he was gone. I never heard from him. I did not know how to find him.' She could not tell her son that he had been utterly indifferent even to the thought of her pregnancy. She shielded him from that rejection. She could only say that she had decided to leave university to have her baby and bring him up. 'Your grandparents helped as much as they could, but they found it difficult. They had put everything into my education, you see, and they were bitterly disappointed that I had to leave university.'

Tony moved uncomfortably, leaning against the kitchen door. 'Okay,' he said. And then, 'Thanks, Mum.' Then he nodded, dismissively, and began to walk to the door. Then, 'Did he have a name, this, this boyfriend of yours?'

'Fadel,' she said. For more than thirteen years it had been unspoken, even in her mind. 'Fadel Ghassan.'

Looking back she could see that from that day something had filtered into their relationship. A chill. An undertone of unspoken things. A separation. She struggled to mend it, and perhaps he did too, but the old delight and openness had gone. For him, the discovery of an enigmatical father and of his mother's affair with him fused with all the burgeoning sense of sex and guilt and pleasure that eroded his days and nights as he grappled with his own sexual awakening and his quest for his identity. It mingled with videos and images on the internet, the seduction of magazines, hot whispered conversations amongst friends at break and lunchtime and glimpses of breast and thigh as the local girls' school boarded the bus. By some dreadful alchemy within his mind, the unattainable bodies of girls and their incessant temptation became confused with his mother, with her easy surrender - and then the words swiftly altered of themselves - her seduction of his father. She, not he, had corrupted the relationship, had given herself away to him, drawing him away from the inherent goodness of his name and dignity. He looked up the meaning of his father's name, "honourable", and it confirmed his fantasy. The compelling, irrational alchemy of adolescence transformed the base to gold, the gold to base. He began to live an existence of intense secrecy, in a world quite separate from his mother, although meeting to eat, pass the essential commonplaces of the day, accept, expect that his washing and ironing would there each morning and food and money always provided. He never touched her now. He never looked to see that she was older, saddened, strained with the care of him, with the ceaseless beating of her mind against the closed door of his life.

Their lives were lived in parallel, through months which became years. Late at night she occasionally heard gobbets of word and rhythm that slammed into the air in the brief moments when he detached his headphones carelessly from his computer. In those seconds, she felt the sound tear into her chest and dislocate her breathing. All that he did, he did in secret now. A job at the supermarket gave him money to spend or save: she did not know. When she went to his bedroom door, she found it locked against her. Sometimes his coldness made her afraid. How could this, her child, so adored, have become so alien, so forbidding?

Some days, returning home from after school classes, he would find her back from work, her head on her arms on the table, the preparation left undone, the dinner not ready and a glass of wine beside her. When she lifted her head to greet him, her eyes were drowsed with tiredness and her speech slow and clumsy. He despised her. He set himself the goal of success at school, competitive, ambitious, obsessional, alone. In the evenings he retreated to his room to study before he played intense, increasingly aggressive Play Station games, or searched the internet for images of sex or violence that would gratify the hungers that had awoken in him. When, two years later, she pulled herself back from the edge of alcoholism and struggled to re-orientate her life, he barely noticed. And as she found kindness and encouragement and a growing relationship with one of the teachers at the school where she worked, he was sullen and unwelcoming. In his final year in the sixth form she introduced David to him as her future husband, a step-father. Sometimes he stayed overnight. They went away together for weekends. Tony saw her behaviour only through the eyes of judgement: loathing for the man who had come into her life; contempt for her, whose willingness to take another partner could only be seen as a kind of promiscuity. A betrayal of the man she had deceived and (he now believed) driven from her; a man he idealised and whose footsteps he would seek in some way to follow as he went to university in the autumn. Once he had left, he would not return. He planned his future carefully, excluding her. Breaking all ties. He would get work to carry him through the holidays so that he need never return in dependence to her.

As the years of his university course passed, sometimes his

mother wrote to him or tried to ring him, but his replies, brusque, careless, repelled her. Her new husband saw her pain, and was helpless to ease it. Then her son had graduated and left university without returning to see them. The last they heard from him that summer had been a brief postcard from a resort in Turkey. He said only that he had an internship waiting for him in a Dorset town, far away from what had once been his home.

***

So, it had not been difficult to identify him in those early weeks of term and ensure that gradually, discreetly, over the coming months and then the years of his course he was ensnared, a limed bird who thought that he had found the freedom of flight. They waited, drawing him carefully through the outer circles of a generous and sincere religious devotion into the centre of their fanaticism. As he was drawn more closely in, he spoke of changing his name, perhaps even taking his father's. A sign of intense devotion, of a new identity. No, they told him. Your current name, your passport, are invaluable to us. Your devotion is known. Let this be an act of sacrifice. In late June, the summer of his graduation, he was sent on his first mission.

The route was easy for him, secure, unquestioned on his British passport. He appeared to travel with a group of holiday makers, tickets booked for the resort of Marmaris in Turkey. He was told to attach himself unobtrusively to them as they made their way to the ticket desk at the airport and then through passport control. No-one questioned a young man, so clearly a member of a party of other young men and women, students probably, on their way to the sun. But at Dalaman airport he stepped aside: away from the groups of collegiate laughter and the families pushing young children in buggies and older couples struggling to fetch their luggage from the belt. He shouldered his rucksack and walked to the waiting taxi rank. There would be a sign, he was told. Unmistakeable. And there was. A name. A greeting. A handclasp of brotherhood and then he was driven through palm-lined streets of white hotels and apartments and glimpses of waiting sun beds in rows around brilliant pools. He saw their luxury with contempt, relieved to turn from the dazzle of white and turquoise blue to the shade and dust of streets that led rapidly away from the town. Winding roads that led up into the mountains; a long drive, stopping briefly once to relieve himself and to be given water and fruit by women who hid their faces decently behind their veils and spoke only in response to the words of his driver. Then driving on, east, climbing the rough, half-made roads, avoiding the main route to Antalya until, exhausted, he found himself in a remote village as night was falling. The darkness was still hot with the burning of the day and stabbingly bright with stars. There they stopped to eat and sleep and he was greeted as a brother by those who would assist the devout to fight in a holy struggle. Then the next day, gruelling miles on foot, treading ancient herdsmen's paths. Each step of hardship was a strange perverse gratification, leading him across the border in secret to join the army.

He had, in those first secret weeks of camp life, been used in menial tasks, digging for the essential latrines, cleaning, cooking and later digging the pits far beyond the camp that buried the desecrated bodies of captives. His days were relieved only by weapon training. They were tasks designed to break him into an unquestioning and deadened obedience until he was called on to prove himself by acts of cruelty and torment. Acts that were to be performed on prisoners, on women and children, on those of racial or religious difference, all who could not flee. His leaders watched him constantly, saw his usefulness, the easily accessed hatreds that fuelled him, his impervious treatment of those weaker than himself. His passionate, relentless devotion. They saw that he fed avidly upon each act of discipline that was required of him, from the most menial to the most brutal, and emerged from each hungry for the next, as though it were a necessity of life. He took part in the ravaging destruction of ruins that had once been ancient colonnades of calm beauty, temples of timeless piety. He fought, briefly, in the wreckage of what had once been a living village. Now it was a desolation of devastated houses, their furnishings shattered. The secrets of bed and kitchen were exposed and broken open, just as the women and children lay askew, bloodied and disjointed in the roofless rooms. Outside, the quiet gardens were shredded, and the crops and animals taken or destroyed. The men, fighting and struggling, had been captured and shot, those who were fortunate. Others had been forced to watch the hacking apart of all that they had loved. He remembered still, not in his conscious mind, but in his hands and nerves, the resistance of bone and tendon, the effusion of blood and its stench in the hot sun. Sometimes he awoke to that memory, as though in sleep his hands remembered what his mind denied, and re-enacted the stab and tug of the knife, and he felt again the sticky lacquer of blood on his hands and wrists.

But he was too valuable to be expended on war. They called for him, taking him on long night-time journeys over rutted and grinding roads through checkpoints and barricades. At first they asked him to work with their engineers, supervising the slave labour that dug the clandestine tunnels that threaded beneath the cities they captured. He checked for signs of collapse, for changes in the structure of the rock, the composition of the soil that would threaten the stability of this secret labyrinth. But as he proved himself, rigid in his careful watchfulness, ruthless in the demands he made on those who laboured naked beneath the surface of the earth, they called for him again.

'You are a surveyor, you say.' They spoke with a grim, shared irony. 'So. We are sending you back. Look for the cracks in the foundations. Subvert, see where you might recruit, wait. Above all wait,' they said to him. 'Conceal yourself. Make no contact with anyone. We will find you. Wait for our call.'

Then he had returned in early October, sent back on the same safe route, smuggled over the border to his waiting brothers, who brought him over remote mountain tracks and roads until he could attach himself to groups of young men and girls at the holiday resort, smiling, sun-tanned as they were. His return ticket was waiting for him, and details of a neighbouring resort to enable him to blend with them. He would walk alongside them, masked by their laughter and reminiscence, through to his flight, yet with his own covert mission to infiltrate, to conceal himself in the most unsuspecting situation, to bring devastation to a complacent and corrupt society. To erode the foundations and bring it down. Wait patiently. You are a virus, they had told him, smiling. And now, to bide his time, working his way into the secure, harmless, conventional job of a surveyor in a small country town.

***

This was his first visit to a client; the first of what he guessed would be many like it. A job for an insurance firm, to confirm that all was secure. He could learn his trade from it, he thought, even from the fussily anxious mentoring of Graham Walker. Deference to him was the perfect concealment. The notes he had about the house cynically amused him as he read them: the traditional building eroded by a flood beneath the main floors and the appended note of the discovery of the long-concealed inseparable skeletons in the cellar. But coming here had not been what he had expected. Not this. Not this encounter with this woman.

As he had got out of the car, he had seen the boy, digging in the garden by the drive, planting bulbs. Daffodils from netted bags, picturing bright gold clusters of stars and trumpets; tulips lying alongside in packets: red, yellow, white; some with fringed-lips and some slashed with green. The boy had barely acknowledged them as they passed him, only nodding, and then quickly bending down to the work. A boy, not much younger than himself, engaged in such a futile task. As if there would ever be a spring!

He had followed Graham, noting the details of the damage, the entry points of the water, then, as they went through the ground floor of the house, the structural work that now reinforced the staircase, the floors and ceilings. He half-listened to the woman as she led them through the house and then brought them to the cellar. Here, if there were a problem, here it would be seen. But he had not expected to be confronted by her trust, her naked assumption that they would share her compassion. Hearing her, watching her, and trapped with her in the confines of this cellar, with its strange quietude, he hated her for her frank and instinctive kinship with the dead, her pity for them. It opened for him memories of nameless deaths that he had witnessed and deaths that he had caused, bodies huddled among anonymous mounds of spoil and rubble beneath hot and stinking skies. The ferrous smell of the bloodied shambles, the stink of harsh sweat in confined spaces, the stench of decay and dissolution, awoke in his nostrils, crawled on his skin. He hated her for this chance encounter that had subverted the very foundations of his being and had released into him an insidious flood of kindness. That had brought perilously near to the surface of his mind an unspeakable question: how did one private hatred become this huge, engorged rage, this ruthlessness? He saw it, momentarily, as a drop of mercury, minute at first, yet gathering others to itself, dissolving, coalescing, into one sated bead of poison. He rubbed his eyes with the back of his hand as though to clear his vision. Watching him, Theresa saw a moment's vulnerability, bewilderment perhaps, almost a child's gesture. Strange, she realised, in this aloof, controlled young man.

'I think of them often,' she said. 'The pity of it.' She smiled at him, seeking to put him at his ease. She stood still, guileless, unthreatening. He glanced again at her careless, casual dress. The jeans, the shirt open at the neck so that he could see the arc of her collar bone, the smooth curve above her breasts. Her hand was touching the wall delicately as though she felt through it some strange communion with the past. She smiled again in innocence, untouched by the darkness that he carried. She did not say how completely this discovery had opened up to her an understanding of herself, both past and future. That was known only to her.

He thought, but only for a second's pulse, what can I do? I cannot turn back and undo the past. I cannot hide anywhere. He knew with terrible certainty that they would find him. There were video images, not used as propaganda on the Internet, but kept he realised now, to hold him as a hostage. I cannot hand myself in. Everything I am today is locked into this identity, this purpose.

Unbidden words came yet again out of a distant classroom. "I am in blood stepped in so far, that turning back were tedious as go o'er." He had not understood then the unspeakable weariness of evil. He understood it now and for a heartbeat could, yet did not, choose the possibility of a different road. Affect threatened him, more dangerous than any weapon; the terror of allowing feeling to re-enter his mind and heart.

His frantic thoughts ran on, each one an instant of vivid perception. He knew that they would send for him. One day, the call. To go to brethren in London or Birmingham, Leicester, Bradford. He did not know where. Nor whether his death would be required in a splintering moment of havoc and terror, or whether it would be the call to war, to bring about the pure kingdom, the undiluted holiness of righteousness, the rule and total conformity. He did not know. Sometimes he imagined the destruction that must make all secure. That would bring the longed for perfection that consumed the core of his being, that drove his secret, devoted prayers. Sometimes he walked the streets near to his office and visualised the walls of Sherborne Abbey blown to dust, its idolatrous carvings, its radiant glass and high branching ceiling, splitting into shards of destruction. Yet in his dreams, uncontrollably, he also saw and heard the fleeing screams of this apostate people as the torrent was unleashed against them, and would awaken gasping for air and light. To force himself away from the danger of his thoughts he looked at her with renewed contempt - the uncovered, freckled arms, the naked, shameless face, fringed by hair that was turning white at the edges as the colour faded from it.

She smiled at him with kindness and he hated her. Hated his

mother in her. Hated her unconscious, indestructible gentleness. Hated the enduring absurdity of love.

Turning from her, he closed his notebook, putting it with his pens and I Pad carefully into the small briefcase he carried, and without waiting or speaking, turned to climb the steps and bow his head under the door lintel to leave. She lingered for a little. Something had changed. Some echo of the raw and despoiling violence that had entered this house centuries ago had entered it again, and violated this space. Some inundation of darkness. She shook such feelings from her. How could it be? She considered the young man she had just spoken to. A pleasant, rather shy and formal young man. And his mentor, over-conscientious, perhaps. She had learned to work with and wait alongside many such in the past, as she had visited properties and paused to hear their ponderous findings. But she could remember how impatient she would feel as her mind was already engaged with the next property, the next visit, whilst they would delay over scrupulous detail. She could sympathise with the young man if he felt that way. Her thoughts now ran on into safer channels. This was a mild, clear autumn morning, and they had the steady expectation that the surveyor would tell them that all was well, and the foundations of their home secure. The winter need hold no anxiety for them.

She said again to herself, 'Love is at the roots of this house.' Then, as if compelled, fiercely, whispering aloud, 'Love. It is indestructible.' She left the cellar, turning back once to look with something like reverence at the shelf where such a timeless offering of love had laid. The quietness surged back to fill the space again.

Very soon, the surveyor and his young intern left, slamming the heavy car doors.

'Your report, Mrs Henley,' Graham Walker said, leaning

out of the car window and looking up at her before starting the engine. The young man sat still beside him, not even glancing up, his eyes focused on his hands as he adjusted the seat belt and then checked his phone. 'I don't foresee any problems. It should be with you and the insurer in a matter of days and then the last of the work can be completed.'

He smiled at her, while the young man sat beside him unmoving, aware only of the vital need to recover his rigid purpose of hate, of the silent, unquestioning discipline of waiting for the chosen time, whenever it might be. The message that would come to him one day. A stranger in the street. An innocently coded email. A text on the mobile phone that waited otherwise unused beside his bed: "Now. Come". And their instructions.

As she waited, Theresa spoke words of thanks, of farewell, to both. Then the surveyor turned the key in the ignition and she stood back as they backed and swung neatly around to drive away.

She remained motionless for a few moments, her hand still raised to wave to them as they left. Then she turned as Adam stood up, his knees stiffened with the work of planting. He rubbed them ruefully, half-laughing and came to be beside her and they watched the car go down the lane. The afternoon had turned away from brightness while the men had been here, and now she felt the cold and the diminishing of the sun. They stood together silently.

She spoke to him after a while. 'We must start to plant the orchard, Adam. Apples, pears. Perhaps peaches would grow along a southern wall. We have time before the winter, before the frosts.'

He nodded. It was always hard for him to begin to say what had been gathering in his mind, but when he spoke it was with an undertone of confident, shared laughter. 'I thought, chickens, Mum! Over there, where we found the remains of old outbuildings. Maybe there.' He pointed across the drive to where there were rough patches of scrub, bramble and nettle and broken wall, lifeless in the shadows. 'Chickens. We could build a shed and make sure the foxes can't get in, and have a safe yard for them.'

She smiled, nodding, shaking from her the sense of unease that had lingered after she had said goodbye to the surveyor and his intern, unease that seemed strangely akin to this chill, dull light. She momentarily tucked her arm through Adam's, sharing his pleasure. They walked slowly together along the drive, talking contentedly of plans and hopes. And as they walked, he pointed out to her where he had planted bulbs, daffodils and tulips, in the full assurance of spring. Beyond the garden, neglected fields were waiting for cultivation. Towards the lane at the foot of the drive, the pollard willows marked the line of the channel, invisible to them from the house, where the waters lay, sedate and quiet now, their currents leashed in, their banks scoured in readiness for the winter rains.

They reached the little bridge over it and stood to gaze at the water. As always, it reflected back to them only the present, a dull mirror of the sky, the imperceptible movement of clouds, their own bodies leaning over, a seeming stillness amidst the stirring of rushes, leaves and swaying grass.

Yet far beneath this placid surface lay the latent turmoil of waters that waited for the rising of tides far away and the pelting rain of clouds as yet ungathered above distant oceans.

Acknowledgements

Sidney Godolphin, Cavalier Poet, born 1610, died fighting for the Royalist cause at Chagford, Devon, 9th February, 1643. Included are extracts from: *"Cloris, it is not thy Disdain"* and *"Hymn: Lord when the Wise Men came from Far"*. The spelling has been modernised.

Robert Herrick, Poet, Clergyman, 1591 - 1674. Included are references to: *"To Virgins, to Make Much of Time"* and *"Upon Julia's Clothes"*.

William Shakespeare, 1564 - 1616: reference is made to *"The Winter's Tale"*, *"A Midsummer Night's Dream"*, *"Troilus and Cressida"*, *"Hamlet"* and *"Macbeth"*.

Orlando Gibbons, Composer, 1583 - 1625. Reference is made to his Madrigal, *"The Silver Swan"*.

Oliver Cromwell. *Letter to the Honourable William Lenthall, Speaker of the Parliament of England, Dublin, 17th September, 1649.*

The English Civil War, A Military History of the Three Civil Wars 1642 - 1651, by Brigadier Peter Young and Richard Holmes, first published Eyre Methuen Ltd 1974 A rich resource of information about the organisation, equipment and campaigns of the Royalist and Parliamentarian armies.

Lightning Source UK Ltd.
Milton Keynes UK
UKOW05f1652300617
304420UK00001B/20/P

9 781912 192403